The

Saturday

Sixpence

and other tales

a selection of short stories set in a
fictional Scottish seaside town
during the 1960's

James Kingscott

ISBN: 9798556376090

Published by:

Wast-By Books
26 Friday Walk
Lower Largo
Fife
Scotland
KY8 6FB

Contents

	Page
The Saturday Sixpence	7
A Day at the Races	17
Robbie the Railwayman	29
Sammy the Scaffie	39
Auld Alex	53
Comic Singer	65
An Unlikely Hero	77
The Haver	91
The Phantom Car	101
Cutting Off His Nose to Spite His Face	115

1

The Saturday Sixpence

The morning sunshine shone brightly through the small bedroom window and on to the face of the young lad lying curled up in his tangled bedclothes. Young Sandy Smith frowned as the warm rays tickled his nose.

Slowly, he opened his eyes and sat up, struggling at first to focus on his brightly lit environment. A warm smile gradually spread over the youngster's face as he remembered what day it was. Saturday!

Sandy fell back in to bed with a thud and closed his eyes, allowing the feeling of contentment that always accompanied the start of the weekend to soak through his body.

After a minute or so he jumped out of bed and switched on his small transistor radio, flooding the room with the latest pop sounds of the 1960's; the sound of which his father so vociferously disapproved. The youngster climbed back into bed, and snuggled cosily into the blankets as the sound of the latest chart hits blared out of the small, inadequate speaker.

Some mothers and fathers had readily accepted this new type of music to which the 1960's had given birth; others, including Sandy's mum and dad, were still preaching the virtues of the sounds which had flooded the dance halls of the previous decade.

Sandy's hankering for the new fashions and hairstyles that were sweeping through 1960's Britain were always met with the same, predictable response, when he expressed his longing to become part of the new trend.

"You're not going around looking like a wee lassie!", was his father's reply to Sandy's timid request that his short back and sides be replaced with the hairstyle currently donned by his latest pop idol. The suggestion that his next pair of trousers be replaced with a pair of jeans was met with a similar refusal. "Dungarees are for workmen", the young lad had been advised.

Sandy consoled himself with the reflection that he was, after all, now ten years old. He was into double figures. "Just wait 'til ah'm a teenager", he whispered as he pulled the bedclothes tightly around himself; "then ah'll show them!"

Suddenly, the loud and angry voice of his mother rudely awakened the youngster from his trance.

"Sandy! If ye dinnae get up soon it'll be dinner time afore ye've had yer breakfast!"

Sandy jumped out of bed and quickly dressed into the crumpled clothes that lay scattered on the floor of his bedroom, having been sleepily discarded the night before. Reaching the bottom of the stairs, he found that his way was blocked by his mother.

"Have ye washed yersel'?"

"Aye mum".

"Well it disnae look like it tae me. When ye've had yer breakfast I want tae see ye get back up thae stairs an' gie' that neck a scrub".

Sandy entered the kitchen, where his dad was seated behind the pages of the morning newspaper. Pouring himself a large helping of corn flakes covered by a generous splash of milk, over which an entire dessert spoon of sugar was sprinkled, the hungry youngster set about devouring the feast whilst reading the back of the corn flakes packet.

"Sandy!"

Sandy looked up from his plate as he noisily munched on his cereal, and was met with the angry glare of his father peering over his morning paper.

"How many times have I told you about putting too much sugar on your food? You'll get worms! And try not to make so much noise when you're eating".

Parents. Always finding reasons to shout and make a fuss over nothing. Never mind though, it was Saturday. Soon he would escape from this dominated existence into his own weekend world; a world where he was in charge and mothers, fathers and teachers were of little significance.

Sandy raised his bowl and, putting it to his mouth, drained the last few drops of sweet milk from the plate. Jumping up to grab his anorak from its peg on the wall, the young lad escaped out of the back door and headed along the narrow streets of Seadykes, the small fishing town that Sandy had called home ever since he had come into the world just over ten years ago.

Before long he reached his granny's house. Grannies, unlike parents and teachers, were allowed into Sandy's Saturday world. In fact, his granny was a vital ingredient.

"Come in my wee man!" shouted the cheery voice from the scullery, as he closed the heavy front door behind him.

Sandy walked through the living room and entered the small adjoining kitchen, where his gran was seated with a steaming cup of tea.

"Dae ye want your usual?" asked granny, knowing full well what the answer would be.

Granny fetched a banana from the larder and proceeded to mash it to a pulp on a small side plate before placing it in front of the young lad.

Sandy then lifted a teaspoon of sugar from the sugar bowl and sprinkled it over the mashed banana.

Then another. And another. "Aye, ye've a sweet tooth," chuckled gran.

Despite having already consumed a large plateful of corn flakes barely fifteen minutes earlier, the mashed banana hardly touched the sides of Sandy's mouth. Granny watched him lick his plate and knew what was coming next.

"Can I hae my Saturday Sixpence?"

Granny rose and fumbled for her purse in the small drawer in the sideboard. Pressing the small shiny coin into Sandy's hand she said, as she had said every Saturday for as long as he could remember; "now dinnae tell yer Faither! He's aye tellin' me no tae gie ye money for sweeties. What he disnae ken, though, winnae harm him!"

Thanking his gran and promising to keep quiet about his secret pocket money, Sandy headed off to the shops.

Seadykes Shore Street was an extremely busy place on Saturday mornings. On one side of the thoroughfare was an array of small shops selling every kind of thing you could imagine; including a butcher, a baker, and a grocer; all of which were busy with housewives and frustrated mothers going about the business of procuring their weekly errands, with the screams of excited children ringing in their ears. Then there were the shops that Sandy preferred to frequent, such as the toy shop, the sweetie shop and Giovanni's ice cream parlour.

On the other side of Shore Street was the harbour; busy in its own way with fishermen mending nets or taking advantage of the good weather to apply a lick of paint to storm damaged boats, all amidst the stench of empty fish boxes drying in the morning sun.

The morning catch, having been landed in the early hours, had already been transported to the town's railway station, from where the fresh haddock was, by now, well on its way to the markets in the larger towns and cities.

Sandy made his way through the stacks of fish boxes and found his granddad seated on a bench enjoying a pipe and having a crack with some of his fellow senior citizens. With his pipe clenched firmly between his teeth, Sandy's granddad grinned as he approached.

Sandy loved to sit with the old fishermen, and listen to their tales of long ago. Sometimes he would sit for hours listening to their yarns about going to sea in days gone by; about the mischief that they had got up to when they were Sandy's age; when, they assured him, the Summer was longer and the days were much warmer than they were now.

This was Saturday morning, though, and as Sandy had a sixpence burning a hole in his pocket, there were more important matters to be dealt with than listening to his granddad's cronies.

"Hae ye been tae see yer gran?" enquired granddad.

"Aye, and she's gi'en me ma pocket money", replied Sandy.

"Good lad. Dinnae spend it a' in the one shop now, and mind how ye cross that road".

"Aye granddad".

Sandy crossed the busy street and gazed into the sweetie shop window. What could he buy with his sixpence?

Six Penny Dainties? A Monster Bar and three Milk Chews?

What about six sticks of liquorice and a Sherbet Fountain? Or six Black Jacks and a quarter of Cola Cubes?

He could, of course, keep half of the money for a comic and only spend threepence on sweeties.

It was when Sandy was addressing this important but rather pleasant problem that he felt a tap on his shoulder. Turning around, his heart sank when he saw who had been standing behind.

"Hae ye got money for sweets then?" enquired the figure standing before him. Stevie McDonald, a scruffy individual sporting a mop of tousled hair and dressed in tatty clothes that he had long since outgrown, was the last person that Sandy wanted to see right at that particular moment in time.

"No I havnae", replied Sandy.

"But ye aye get a sixpence from your gran on a Saturday", came the reply.

"Well I haven't got one today", said Sandy, struggling to sound truthful. "And anyway, I wouldn't be buying anything for you with it if I did".

"Aw go on!" pleaded Stevie. "I'll be your best pal".

The last person that Sandy wanted for his best pal was Stevie.

His overpowering nature, scruffy appearance and constant lack of pocket money of his own made him about as popular to his school-chums as a force nine gale to a fishing boat at sea.

"Look Stevie, I haven't got any money for sweeties. And anyway, I've to get away home now".

Sandy turned and started to walk back in the direction of his house. He kept on walking until he was sure that Stevie's eyes were no longer following him.

He then turned around and scanned the street to make sure that his unwanted companion was nowhere to be seen, before heading back towards the shops.

Pausing outside Giovanni's ice cream parlour, he pondered over whether or not to spend his money on a cone.

Of course, this choice would result in the entire sixpence being spent on one single item, but then Giovanni's ice cream was the best for miles around and a sixpenny cone was worth every penny!

Turning this latest idea over in his mind as he passed the toy shop, his attention was suddenly diverted to the display in the window. Model aeroplane kits, model ships, toy cars, games. In fact, everything that a young lad could dream of finding in his stocking on Christmas morning was on display. There was nothing in the toy shop window that his Saturday sixpence would stretch to, however, the youngster lamented.

The main focus of his attention at the toy shop, though, was the model train that wound its way through the miniature trees and houses at the front of the window then disappeared into a tunnel at the back of the display before eventually re-emerging at the other side to begin its journey all over again.

As Sandy stood mesmerized, watching the engine continue on its never ending travels, the hypnotic effect was suddenly broken when once again he felt a tap on his shoulder. With a sigh, he turned around expecting to see Stevie, but instead his eyes met with the overpowering figure of his father.

"It's a long time until Christmas, Sandy lad. Anyway, your behaviour will have to improve a long way before you can expect to find anything like that in your stocking!"

"Aye dad, I suppose so", muttered Sandy, thanking his lucky stars that he had not been tucking into a big cone when his father had seen him. That would have given the game away, and his gran would have been in big trouble.

"I'm away for a blether with your granddad", said his father as he crossed the street. "Mind and behave now".

Walking on a little further, Sandy came to the newsagents, where his favourite comic was on display in the magazine rack outside the shop.

Looking inside the shop to make sure that Mr. Brown the newsagent couldn't see him, Sandy removed the comic from the stand and started to read.

This wasn't really stealing, he assured himself. It was more like borrowing. If he could finish reading the comic and replace it in the rack before he was discovered, then no-one would be any the wiser, and his sixpence would still be intact!

But, just when his feasting eyes were devouring the latest adventures of Bruno the Bear, Sandy's luck evaded him once again when an angry voice bellowed from within the shop.

"Put that back afore I kick yer backside!" shouted Mr. Brown from his vantage point behind the counter. "If every laddie in the toon wis tae feast their eyes on my comics for free, then I'd be oot o' business!"

Sandy quickly replaced the comic, and made himself scarce.

The time had come when a decision had to be made. In order to complete the half finished story, Sandy would have to spend half of his money on the comic. This would only leave sufficient funds for three Milk Chews, or one Monster Bar. Or a packet of Potato Puffs.

As he stood in front of the paper shop considering his options in the warmth of the morning sunshine, the young lad's thoughts turned back to the ice cream shop.

The thought of a cone was too much to bear. The sun was now high in the sky, and its heat was beginning to make Sandy sweat inside his anorak. The decision made for him, he promptly about turned and headed back towards Giovanni's. After checking to make sure his dad was nowhere to be seen, he entered the ice cream parlour.

"A sixpenny cone please", he said to the elderly Italian gentleman serving behind the counter.

Giovanni reached for a cone, placed two large dollops of vanilla ice cream on top, then held out his hand.

"That'll be sixpence, please".

Sandy fumbled around in his pocket for his money. He was sure it was in his right hand trouser pocket. Maybe not. He tried his other pocket. No sign of it there either. Perhaps he had put it in his anorak. Sandy searched through all of his anorak pockets in vain.

A queue was now starting to build up in the shop. Impatient customers with parched throats, all desperate to satisfy their desire for an ice cream, were beginning to pass comment.

The sixpence must surely be in his trouser pockets! Sandy searched once again in his right hand pocket, only this time he pushed his hand all the way down as far as it would go.

But there was no sign of his money. Instead of a shiny sixpence, all he found was a hole in the bottom!

"That'll be sixpence", said Mr. Giovanni impatiently, a thin trickle of melting ice cream starting to run over his fingers.

"I've lost my money!" cried Sandy.

He turned and ran out of the shop, staring at the ground as he retraced his steps back along the street.

Every square inch of pavement was covered as the distraught youngster searched in vain, head bowed, for the lost coin.

Sandy's pace quickened as he made his way back towards the newsagents; but instead of his Saturday sixpence, all that came into view as his eyes scoured every nook and cranny on the ground before him was a pair of shoes.

Slowly, Sandy raised his eyes to see who was blocking his path.

Stevie McDonald stood before him; his mouth covered with melting ice cream, which was also beginning to form a small puddle on the ground as it dripped from the cone gripped tightly in his hand.

"Guess what, Sandy," he said. "I found a sixpence!"

2

A Day at the Races

It was the day of the annual Boat Tavern Social Club outing to the horse racing at Castleburgh. All week long, Davie Wilson had been eagerly looking forward to the big day out and, on the morning of the trip, he had risen with the lark, washed and shaved, supped his bowl of porridge, and was now enjoying a cup of tea as he perused the day's race card in the morning paper.

The first race at Castleburgh that afternoon was the 12:40, and Davie scrolled down the list of runners trying to decide which cuddy to back. With the early morning sunshine streaming through the window, his eyes lit up when he saw that one of the runners was called 'Bright Morn'!

The bright rays of sun that were filling the room simply had to be a good-luck omen, and Davie excitedly moistened the tip of his pencil before scribbling the name of the horse in his notebook, along with the time of the race.

The fact that the horse had shown poor form of late, and had been rated as a 40-1 outsider, had absolutely no bearing on his choice. It was a sunny morning and the horse was called 'Bright Morn'. That was good enough for Davie.

Next was the 13:30, and once again the choice for this race was staring out at him. Having nicked his face that morning whilst shaving, it just had to be 'Deep Cut', another outsider that had the questionable honour of being entered into Davie's notebook.

The horses from the remaining four races were chosen in the same manner. There was 'Day Tripper' in the 14:15 (for obvious reasons); 'Red Rose' in the 15:10 (Davie's garden was full of them!); 'Wee Dram' in the 16:00 (he enjoyed the odd nip along with his pint); then, in the 16:45, the big race of the afternoon, 'Daft Davie'!

It has to be said that the choice of this last named nag was rather appropriate. Although never freely admitting to having limitations when it came to making decisions that required a certain degree of intelligence, it was clearly obvious to all and sundry that Davie Wilson was not exactly the brightest light in the harbour.

His denseness had first become apparent as a young laddie at SeadykesPrimary School, where he had found the lessons rather hard to comprehend. His teachers would frequently accuse the youngster of not paying attention, and not listening to what he was being taught.

"What are your ears for, Wilson?" shouted one frustrated teacher, who had just about reached the end of her tether. Davie had looked puzzled, before replying, quite innocently, "erm, for hooking my glasses on to miss?"

Davie was bachelor, and in all probability would always remain so. He had lived all of his thirty-five years in the fishing community of Seadykes, and was an only child. Needless to say, he was his mother's pride and joy. As for his father, who had walked out when Davie was just a young lad, he had only vague memories.

However, although he had never gained even the most basic qualification during his school days, Davie had never wanted for work. On leaving school he had acquired a small boat from which he set creels to catch lobsters and partans (the local name for edible brown crabs).

He also fished for codling using a primitive hand-held fishing line and, during a few weeks in mid-summer, he used that same fishing line to catch mackerel.

All the fish and shellfish that he caught, apart from what he kept back for 'a wee fry' for himself and his mother, was sold to the local fish merchant; the proceeds being a welcome addition to the meagre income his mother earned as a machinist in the local knitwear factory.

Despite the undeniable fact that Davie was regarded by all who knew him as 'not the sharpest knife in the box', he was, nonetheless, a likeable character, who enjoyed nothing better at the weekend than a visit to his local hostelry, the Boat Tavern.

Every Friday and Saturday night, Davie could be seen propping up the bar in 'The Boatie', having a laugh and blether with his chums.

He was also a keen member of the pub's social club, who were responsible for organising the annual outing to the racecourse at Castleburgh. Davie had never missed the annual trip to the races for as long as he could remember!

Davie looked up at the clock on the mantelpiece. It was now nine o'clock, and time to start making his way to the agreed meeting point where the party of day-trippers were to be picked up by local coach-operator Tam Broon and his minibus.

Ten minutes later, Davie stood waiting at the 'bus stop. He had been determined to be first in the queue, so that he could claim the seat directly behind the driver.

Tam Broon, it has to be said, was less than keen on this idea, as the thought of having to endure Davie gibbering in his ear for the entire two-hour journey to Castleburgh was the stuff of nightmares.

At ten minutes to ten, and with Davie still standing alone at the 'bus stop, Tam's mini-bus drew to a halt in front of him. Tam rolled down the driver's window and, in an exasperated voice, announced that one of the tyres was soft.

"I'm going to have to return to the depot to have the wheel changed", said Tam, before adding "I'll be back here in about half-an-hour".

No sooner had the mini-bus disappeared around the corner, than the other passengers started to turn up, and before long the air was filled with excited chatter in eager anticipation of the exciting day out that lay ahead.

The agreed hour of departure came and went. Impatient feet tapped on the footpath, and anxious eyes gazed in the direction from which they expected Tam's mini-bus to appear.

"I hope he's no' been ta'en ill", bemoaned Boat Tavern barmaid Jeannie Smith, who was also secretary and treasurer of the social club, and organiser of the outing.

"Oh, he's no' ill", announced Davie. "He looked perfectly healthy when I saw him earlier this morning".

"You saw him earlier did ye? Why did ye no' say! And did Tam say anything significant when he spoke tae ye?" enquired Jeannie.

"Anything sig .. signif … er, no, ah dinnae think so", replied Davie.

Five more minutes passed as the intending passengers waited impatiently at the kerbside.

"Davie, are ye sure Tam didn't say anything of significance?" Jeannie asked again.

"Did he say anything of signi .. signific .. er, naw."

Another five minutes passed.

"Look Davie, did Tam say anything at all tae ye?"

"Oh, aye", says Davie, "he said the mini-bus had a soft tyre and he was away tae get it sorted. Said he'd be aboot half-an-hour".

"Oh, for crying out loud", screeched Jeannie, "had ye nae idea what the word 'significant' meant? Oh, God give me strength!"

Despite this reprimand, Davie took no offence. He had known Jeannie for years through her job as the Boat Tavern barmaid, and she had said far worse to him in the past. Despite her sharp tongue, Jeannie had a heart of gold, and had it not been for the effort she put in organising the event and gathering the weekly subscription to fund the annual outing, there would probably be no day out at the races.

Tam and his fellow regulars at 'The Boatie' faithfully paid Jeannie sixpence every week throughout the year, which accumulated into sufficient funds to pay for the mini-bus to convey the day trippers to and from Castleburgh, their entry to the race track, and a fish supper on the way home.

Eventually, the replacement vehicle with Tam Broon at the wheel came into sight and drew to a halt. Spirits restored, the excited passengers clambered aboard, and the mini-bus finally got on its way.

In the rush to board, however, Davie failed in his bid to claim the seat behind the driver, and was jostled to the back row, where he found himself seated beside Johnny Hastie and Andy Paterson, both of whom were self-proclaimed 'experts' when it came to picking winners at horse racing events.

Davie listened intently as the two authorities compared notes. Both men had spent hour upon hour studying the race cards; with influential factors such as past form, track condition, the horses' weights and who would be riding them all taken into account.

Davie pretended to understand the conversation, and contributed with the odd "aye that's right", and a nod of the head where appropriate.

"So, have you decided on which runners to back, Davie?" enquired Johnny.

"Aye, that I have", replied Davie.

"And just how did you decide who the likely winners are going to be?" asked Andy, at the same time giving Johnny a nudge. Both men knew that Davie hadn't the foggiest idea about how to pick a winner by using the conventional methods, and both were keen to indulge in a little ribbing, at the same time eager to impart their 'superior' knowledge on all things horse-racing.

"Oh, I got some red-hot tips from a mate with 'insider knowledge'", lied Davie, keen not to let on how he had actually picked his horses.

Just over two hours later, the mini-bus drew into the car park at Castleburgh race track, and the day-trippers poured out before excitedly making their way towards the entrance.

With the first race due to start in around half-an-hour, they would have just enough time to push through the crowds and place their bets before 'the off'.

Once inside, Davie soaked up the atmosphere, and listened to the shouts of the bookmakers, all of whom were claiming to offer the best deals.

He pulled his notebook from his inside pocket and confirmed that his choice for the first race was 'Bright Morn', before pushing his way through to the nearest bookie to place two shillings 'on the nose'.

The bookmaker tried not to smile as he handed Davie his ticket. With the odds having now gone out to 50-1, surely this was the easiest two bob he would ever make!

The race started bang-on 12:40, and Bright Morn, initially, was right up there in the leading pack. Slowly but surely, however, the horse dropped back down the field and, when the winner eventually crossed the line, Davie's choice was nowhere to be seen.

As there was then some time to kill before the second race, Davie decided to treat himself to a hot-dog, and as he waited it the queue at the refreshment kiosk he was spotted by Johnny and Andy, the self-proclaimed 'expert' pundits.

"How did your 'red-hot tip' get on then, Davie? Was that the one bringing up the rear?" Andy enquired mockingly.

"No, that wisnae ma horse", lied Davie.

"Mine wis the one that stumbled at the last fence and wis just pipped at the post".

"Aye, we believe ye", chuckled Johnny, "thousands widnae", and the pair sauntered off.

Once the hot dog had been scoffed, and the tomato sauce had been wiped from his mouth on to the back of his sleeve, Davie made his way back to the bookies' stalls, and placed two shillings on 'Deep Cut', his second choice.

This time, however, he had decided to 'play it safe', and placed an each-way bet; which, at odds of 30-1, would guarantee a return of seventeen shillings if the horse finished in the first three.

If the horse won the race, though, his winnings would be almost four pounds. A fortune!

Quietly confident, Davie looked on as the race got under way, but sadly it was a similar story to the first race.

His choice started reasonably well, but eventually fell back before finishing second last.

Ever the optimist, however, Davie was encouraged by the fact that the horse hadn't been the last to cross the line, and surely this was a sign that his fortunes were about to improve!

Alas, it was the same story with his next three selections; 'Day Tripper', 'Red Rose' and 'Wee Dram'.

"Aye", Davie lamented as the last named nag crossed the line well behind the rest of the field; "ah could do wi' a wee dram mysel' right now!"

A total of ten shillings, a huge portion of Davie's earnings for the week, had now been handed over to the bookies with not a penny coming in the other direction.

All his hopes were now pinned on 'Daft Davie', his choice of runner for the last race on the day's card.

Davie approached the bookmakers' stalls, and observed that 'Daft Davie' was being offered at 25-1, much shorter odds than his previous choices that afternoon, but a price that would still pay out handsomely.

Undeterred by his previous failures, he placed his biggest wager of the afternoon, five shillings on the nose!

Bet placed, Davie sought out the best vantage point, which once again just happened to be right next to those knowledgeable pundits, Johnny Hastie and Andy Paterson.

"Well then Davie", enquired Johnny, "what old nag has your imaginary 'mate' with 'insider knowledge' told you to waste your money on this time"?

"If ye must know", replied Davie, "my money's on 'Daft Davie'".

Johnny and Andy simultaneously burst into peals of laughter.

"You're havin' us on, surely?" sniggered Andy. "That horse hasnae a snowball's chance in hell! The name's appropriate, though, don't you think Johnny"?

At this, the pair both erupted into fresh guffaws of laughter, and tears of mirth flowed down their cheeks.

"Well, we'll see", Davie replied indignantly. "And seeing as you two are the so-called experts, which horses have you backed?"

"There was only one horse worth backing", advised Johnny, adopting a superior tone. "We both plumped for the favourite, 'Piledriver', which we backed at 3-2 before the odds shortened to evens. It's a dead cert., so much so that we've both wagered a pound on the nose. Nae other runner will hae a look in!"

At precisely 16:45, the starter dropped his flag, the starting rope was raised, and the twelve horses competing in the big race of the afternoon thundered off down the track towards the first fence. All cleared the first hurdle with ease.

'Piledriver', just like the so-called experts predicted, looked strong and invincible as it led the field. 'Daft Davie', however, belied his long odds, and moved up to just a couple of lengths behind the leader as the race progressed.

"Aye, no' sae daft as ye think", boasted Davie.

"He'll never last the pace", retorted Andy.

The challenge of the outsider, however, gradually waned as the race progressed, and the smile was slowly wiped from Davie's face. Going into the last, 'Daft Davie' was bringing up the rear, and both Andy and Johnny turned to look at their despairing chum with looks on their faces that simply said "told you so!"

Their choice, the bookies' favourite, had led from the start, and it was now several lengths ahead. All it had to do was to clear the final fence, then it was an easy canter home to win the race. It was at this point it became clear that there is no such thing as a 'dead cert.'

For some inexplicable reason, 'Piledriver', who had looked so confident throughout the race, clipped the final hurdle and fell.

The chasing pack, which consisted of every horse in the race except for 'Daft Davie', followed the leader over the fence, and every single one of them either met the same fate as 'Piledriver', or dismounted its jockey.

When Davie Wilson realised what had happened, he was grinning from ear to ear.

The rank outsider he had backed was so far behind the pack that his jockey had plenty of time to steer his mount around the pile-up when negotiating the final fence.

Once clear of the last hurdle, 'Daft Davie' had an easy canter to the finish line.

With a smug look on his face, Davie Wilson turned round to face his chums, but they were nowhere to be seen. It had all been too much to take, and the pair had vanished into the crowd before Davie could gloat at them.

"Oh, ye of little faith", he chuckled as he made his way towards to bookie's stall, where he found he was the only punter on the race track to collect winnings on the final race.

"Well done you", congratulated the bookie as he handed over six pounds and ten shillings.

The smile on the turf accountant's face was on a par with Davie's, as the unexpected win for the outsider meant a big payday for him as well!

When Davie arrived back at the mini-bus, he found the other day-trippers were already on board, and keen to start the long journey home.

The only seat left on the coach, however, was nowhere near Andy and Johnny; the pair having no doubt managed to get themselves as far away from the only remaining seat in order to avoid Davie's gloating.

Pleased with how the day had turned out in the end, Davie drifted off into a contented sleep as the mini-bus travelled back up the coast towards Seadykes.

An hour later, he was awakened by a nudge. "Was it a fish supper or a pudding supper you ordered Davie?" asked Jeannie.

"A fish supper with everything on it", replied Davie, as he shook himself awake before taking the tightly-wrapped parcel from her.

He opened out the package, and the aroma of freshly fried haddock and chips, smothered in brown sauce, salt and vinegar filled his nostrils. His mouth watered as he took his first bite of the crisply-battered fish.

"Mmmm, almost as good as winning the 16:45", he chuckled to himself.

The mini-bus started up again, and driver Tam Broon pulled back out on to the main road for the final leg of the journey.

It was at this point that club secretary and treasurer Jeannie, who had been looking after the 'kitty' all day, stood up to make an announcement.

"Can I have your attention", she shouted from the front of the coach.

"Now we've all had a grand day out; we've all had an enjoyable time at the race track; and we've all had our tea from the fish and chip shop."

"However, when all is said and done, we're showing a deficit of seven shillings and sixpence. What do you think we should do?"

There was an awkward silence, before Davie, after swallowing his last piece of fish, shouted from the back: "Ach, I say just gie' it tae the driver".

3

Robbie the Railwayman

Robbie Bowman stirred and opened his eyes. Had the alarm sounded, or was it just part of his dream? He rolled over and looked at the bedside clock. Five past five. Yes, it must have been the alarm he had heard.

With a little effort, Robbie raised himself up to sit on the edge of the bed, where he briefly composed himself before attempting to stand up and move his sixty-five-year-old bones in the direction of the bathroom.

"This is the final time", he told himself as he turned on the tap and filled the sink with water; at the same time allowing himself a wry smile. After today, there would be no more early rises. After today, he would be a man of leisure. Because this was the day that Robert Bowman was finally due to retire from almost fifty years working on the railway.

It was not long after the First World War, 1919 to be precise, that Robbie had first started work with the railway company, the North British it was at that time, as a porter at Seadykes railway station. He loved his job from the very start; handling the loading and unloading of baggage and parcels from the trains, and assisting less able-bodied passengers to board and disembark.

After a few years, Robbie decided that the time was right to better himself, and duly set about gaining the required qualifications and training in order to achieve his dream of becoming a railway guard.

His dream was eventually realised at the age of twenty-five. Ever since then, he had gone about his duties conscientiously, and had often been praised for his attention to detail.

But today that career was to come to an end. Although he was sad that he was leaving the job he loved, he was also glad that he would no longer have to rise at 5am. That part of the job had been getting harder and harder of late!

After having washed, shaved and dressed, Robbie made his way downstairs and put the kettle on the gas stove.

One piece of bread under the grill would suffice. He had little appetite at this time of the morning, and he knew that he would be able to have a nibble from his piece box in the guard's brake van once the early morning train was under way.

Once the kettle had boiled, Robbie made up a large pot of tea, and allowed it to mask whilst he made up some sandwiches for his piece. He filled out a cup of tea, then poured the rest into his flask.

With his cup of tea and slice of toast, Robbie sat at the kitchen table and looked out over the town, where the church steeple was silhouetted against the early morning light. The birds were just starting to sing. It was a peaceful and thought-provoking perspective.

Having to get up at this time in the morning does have its advantages, he reflected, as he sipped the warming tea and nibbled on his toast.

After draining the dregs from his cup, Robbie stood up and donned his railwayman's jacket, grabbed his piece box and flask, then slipped out of the front door before making his way to Seadykes railway station, a mere ten-minute walk away.

The early morning mixed goods train, which was due to depart at 6:30, was sitting in a siding when Robbie arrived at the yard. The engine, with driver Norrie Robertson and fireman Frankie Dewar on the footplate, had arrived a couple of hours earlier, with a few wagons of coal destined for the local Seadykes coal merchant. The engine had then been spun around on the turntable and coupled up to the empty coal wagons that were to be taken back to Wastby, a coal-mining conurbation that lay fifteen miles to the west, along with a parcels van and a fish van.

One solitary fish van. My, how things had changed!

The fish traffic that had been departing from Seadykes station in recent years had been getting much less frequent. Back in the 1930's, when the local herring fishing had been at its height, several fully-laden fish trains could be seen departing from Seadykes every day. Nowadays, with the herring having long since departed from the local fishing grounds, and with road transport starting to take over, it was no longer possible to justify dedicated fish trains. All fish vans, which these days carried only white fish such as haddock or cod, were now coupled to the daily 'mixed' goods service that departed from the coastal town every morning, such as the one that Robbie was about to guard.

Norrie the driver and Frankie the fireman loved doing the coast run. Once they had completed their duties after arriving at Seadykes, if there was time to spare, they would have a quick wander down to the harbour to have a search through the supposedly empty fish boxes for any fish that might have been overlooked. Any they found were taken back up to the goods yard, where they were roasted whole on the fireman's shovel, placed in the engine's fire box, for breakfast.

Norrie and Frankie were tucking in to such a delicacy when Robbie arrived.

"Anyone at home?" he shouted.

"Och, it's yerself, Robbie", Norrie shouted down from the cab. "Here, would ye like some freshly cooked haddock?"

"No, ye're all right", replied Robbie. "I've not long since had a cup of tea and a slice of toast. I'll away and check the train and get the lamps lit on the brake van. This'll be the last time, too. Have ye heard I'm retiring today?"

"Yes, that we have", replied Frankie. "It's a sad day for us as well. We're going to miss you, pal!"

Robbie walked back down the train checking the wagons and brakes before arriving at the guard's wagon, where he pulled himself up on to the veranda, and entered the van.

Taking a bottle of paraffin from the store cupboard, he filled the front, side and tail lamps, lit the wicks, then returned outside to hang the lamps in their appropriate positions.

This was a very important job. During the hours of darkness, or if the train was in a long tunnel, as long as the driver could look back and still see the lamp on the front of the brake van, he knew the train was intact.

Similarly, when the train passed a signal box, the red tail lamp was an indication to the signalman that no wagon had become detached!

Once the lamps had been hung, all that Robbie had to do was wait until the train was ready to depart.

At precisely 6:30, driver Norrie Robertson sounded his whistle and looked back down the train towards Robbie, who was standing out on the brake van's veranda, and signalled that they were ready to depart.

Slowly, the engine edged forwards, and took up the strain. Once all the wagons and the brake van had started to move, Robbie signalled forward to the driver that it was now safe for the engine to pick up speed, and the train started to accelerate out of the yard.

After being jostled as the brake van passed through the points at the throat of the goods yard and on to the main line, Robbie went back inside. Although he would still have to be 'on guard', and keep a constant check on the train from inside the van, Robbie was now able to have a quick cup of tea from his flask.

Ten minutes later, they arrived at Toreness, where they were to couple up to some empty coal wagons and a freight van. After being shunted into a siding, the rake of wagons and brake van were uncoupled from the engine, the new wagons were then shunted into position, and the train was re-assembled.

This operation, which was carried out under Robbie's watchful eye, had to be thought out and executed very carefully. Just under an hour later, the train was ready to depart once again.

The largely uneventful journey from Toreness to Wastby, during which the train had to occasionally wait in a siding to allow a faster service to pass, took about ninety minutes.

As the gradient was against the train for almost the entire journey, there was no need for Robbie to operate the brakes; and, as it was a pleasant June morning, he ventured out on to the brake van's veranda to enjoy the early-morning sunshine and the fresh air.

He was going to miss mornings like these, watching the world go past. The cows were grazing in the fields, and the farm hands, busily going about their business, would occasionally look up and wave as the train steamed past.

It was a different story in winter, of course, when the stove in the brake van had to be lit as soon as Robbie arrived at the station, in order to stave off the bitter cold!

During those cold, dark months, he was content to remain inside for most of the journey and keep an eye on the train through the front window, or from the small lookout positions or 'duckets' that were built into the sides of the brake van.

At ten-past-nine the train arrived at the marshalling yard at Wastby, where the task of uncoupling the wagons was undertaken. This was a time-consuming procedure, where the wagons had to be marshalled into various sidings, from where they would eventually proceed to their ultimate destination. Once this task was done, the three railwaymen headed towards the yard bothy for a well-earned break.

"How will you be filling your days from now on?" enquired Norrie, before taking a noisy slurp from his cup of tea.

"I'm thinking about getting myself a wee boat" replied Robbie. "I've always had a notion to do a bit of fishing. And then there's my wee garden. To be honest, though, it's not very big, and doesn't take a lot of looking after".

"Maybe you could get an allotment?" suggested Frankie.

"Aye, that might be an idea" said Robbie. "That would certainly keep me busy!"

Half-an-hour later, Robbie announced that it was time for him to join the train he would be guarding on the journey back down to Seadykes. With Norrie and Frankie insisting that he look in on them from time to time, Robbie bade the driver and fireman farewell and headed off across the tracks.

It was approaching eleven o'clock when the engine and its small rake of wagons headed out of the Wastby marshalling yard, through the junction, and back down the coast line.

Not long after leaving the yard, on the outskirts of Wastby, the train passed a school, where Robbie observed the children enjoying various playground games; probably the same games that he had played as a young laddie.

He allowed his mind to drift back to those now seemingly far-off childhood days.

With his two school chums, Billy and Ronnie, he would run around the playground at break times laughing and screaming and doing the sort of things that young laddies do. Then, school over for the day, the three pals would go home, get changed into their 'playing clothes', and head off for the seashore, where they would sail their home-made boats in the rock pools until dusk. Yes, those were the days.

The train reached the top of Milton Bank, and for the next two miles Robbie would have to be on his guard, and be ready to apply the brakes if required. As the engine was only hauling six wagons of coal, however, it was unlikely that his assistance would be needed.

The engine reached the bottom of the incline, then steadily started to pull away along the level. Robbie looked out from his veranda as the train wound its way around the edge of a small village and, looking down from his vantage point as they passed the village church, he observed a wedding taking place.

The scene sent his mind wandering once again; back to the early 1920's; back to the day when he had wed his childhood sweetheart.

Robbie and Sandra had known each other for as long as they could remember. They had both went to the same school, the same church, and the same Sunday school. Then, when Sandra had started singing in the church choir, Robbie decided that he, too, would join, under the pretence that he needed a hobby to while away the long winter evenings.

The truth of the matter was that he had always had a fancy for young Sandra, and it soon became apparent that the feeling was mutual. Before long, they started courting, and a short time later their engagement was announced.

"It's a match made in heaven" commented one churchgoer, as she observed the happy couple sitting side by side at the

Sunday morning service. "Aye, they were made for each other, were they not", came the reply.

Robbie and Sandra were married not long after, and their matrimony turned out to be everything they had hoped for. They were eventually blessed with two children, Susan and Tommy; and Robbie was the happiest man alive!

Before he knew it, however, the years had flown by, and Susan and Tommy had flown the nest. Both were now happily married, but had been forced to move far away from Seadykes, where jobs had become increasingly difficult to come by, in order to forge their careers.

Just under an hour later, the train arrived at St. Dronans, where two of the fully-laden coal wagons were to be dropped off. The rake of wagons, including Robbie's brake van, was shunted into a siding, where the engine and first two wagons were uncoupled. The engine then shunted the two wagons into another siding, before returning to be re-attached to the four remaining wagons plus the brake van.

Once complete, the train was able to continue on down the line to Toreness, where the same operation was carried out. Finally, what remained of the train of wagons embarked on the final leg of its journey to Seadykes.

As they approached their final destination, Robbie looked out from the brake van once again, just as they were passing the cemetery on the outskirts of the town.

The cemetery where, just over a year ago, Robbie had bid a tearful final farewell to Sandra, his wife of forty-four years.

It had all happened so quickly. They had both been so looking forward to Robbie's retirement, and had been excitedly planning how they were going to spend their days of leisure.

Visits to both children and their families were on the agenda, and Robbie and Sandra were looking forward to seeing their grandchildren, who they hadn't seen since the previous Christmas.

Then, suddenly, Sandra had passed away without warning. The doctor had explained everything at the time, but Robbie just couldn't take it in. Apparently Sandra had had a condition all of her life that could have killed her at any time.

Perhaps he should just be grateful that they had enjoyed so many happy years together before her unseen illness took its toll. Now, the retirement that he thought was going to be so full of joy and happiness, spent in the company of his beloved Sandra, looked like it was going to be a lonely existence.

The engine slowed as it approached Seadykes station, before entering the goods yard. Once the coal wagons had been shunted into a siding and uncoupled, the engine was attached to a rake of empties for the journey back to Wastby. Robbie lifted his piece box and flask from the brake van, climbed down from the veranda, and said goodbye to the crew. His final day as a railway guard was over.

It was with a tinge of sadness that Robbie made his way over the tracks towards the station buildings, where he would sign off for the last time. He wanted to go without any fuss, and was hoping he could just do the needful before slipping away un-noticed. However, that wasn't how things turned out.

Waiting inside the building for him were several of his colleagues, and standing at the front was the station manager, George Henderson, who stepped forward to shake Robbie's hand.

"We just couldn't let you walk away without a token of our appreciation for all your hard work over the years, Robbie", he said before handing over a small oblong-shaped box.

Robbie opened the box to find it contained a gold watch, suitably inscribed to commemorate his many years of devotion to the railway company. He didn't know what to say, and felt the tears starting to well up in the corner of his eyes.

"And that's not all", said Jimmy Swanston, the porter, as he handed Robbie a small bag. Robbie looked inside the bag and found a small garden trowel and fork.

"We thought" announced Jimmy, "That the station garden needed a bit of looking after. As you're going to have time to spare, maybe you could come and visit your old pals and do a bit of gardening at the same time?"

A huge smile broke out across Robbie's face. His dread of the long, lonely days that he had feared were going to dominate the remainder of his life diminished in an instant.

"Oh, aye" said Robbie, his voice quivering ever so slightly with emotion.

"Aye, I'd like that very much!"

4

Sammy the Scaffie

It was difficult to say exactly when Sammy Scott's life had started to go downhill. It may have been when he was 'taken under the wing' of local spinster Beatrice Blair, almost ten years his senior; it may have been the night he eventually gave in to her advances and, in doing so, rendered her 'with child'; or it may have been the day that, in order to 'do the proper thing', he and Beattie had tied the knot in the local church?

One thing was absolutely certain. At a time in his life that should have been exciting and full of promise for the future, Sammy's fortunes had taken a downward spiral, and he was now what could only be described as a 'hen pecked' husband.

Born less than a year after his father had returned from fighting in the Great War, Sammy's childhood had been a relatively uneventful one. He had never liked school and, being basically a timid and shy sort of laddie, childhood friends had been few and far between.

After finishing his education at the age of fourteen, Sammy had taken up employment in his father's joinery workshop; his dad having set up the business shortly after being discharged from the army.

It was a situation that had suited Sammy. He no longer had to endure the torture of the class room and the constant threat of the tawse; and the meagre allowance his father paid him was more than enough pocket money for a youngster who had few interests outside his immediate family environment.

Young Sammy had little interest in the fairer sex during those early years; and, in any case, his bashful nature would have hindered rather than helped any possible romance blossoming.

He was a good-looking laddie, though; and, as he rapidly developed from a gangly youth to an attractive young man, more than a few appreciative glances had been cast in his direction from female admirers.

One such admirer was Beatrice Blair, or 'Beattie' as she was more commonly known, who lived alone in the flat above the Scotts. As Sammy had been maturing into a rather handsome seventeen-year-old, she would often peer out from behind her curtains to ogle at the rapidly developing youth as he worked in his father's yard.

Beatrice was now well into her twenty-seventh year and, so far, romance seemed to have eluded her. As the months and years passed, she had become more than a little anxious that she may be forever a spinster, and was terrified of the possibility that she could end up being 'left on the shelf'.

As well as having this yearning for romance, Beattie also suffered from loneliness, with both of her parents having passed away at a relatively young age. She craved companionship; someone to sit with her in the evenings. But all she had for company was her collection of romantic novels.

The main problem with Beatrice, however, was not that she was physically unattractive. In fact, quite the opposite was true. No, the reason that Beattie had so far failed to get 'hitched' was entirely down to her dominating nature.

She may not have even realised it herself, but any prospective boyfriends she had tried to procure over the years had found her personality so intimidating that any possible relationship had been snuffed out before it had even started.

It was rather ironic, therefore, when that same intimidating personality, coupled with Sammy's reticent nature, resulted in an intimacy that was, in a very short time, to have far-reaching consequences.

It was a hot and sunny afternoon when, on a half-day holiday from her job as a shop assistant in the local co-operative store, Beattie had opened the window and called down to Sammy to enquire if he would like a cool glass of lemonade.

Sammy, who was working bare-chested in the warm sunshine, and with a mouth as dry as a whistle, gratefully accepted the offer.

To cut a long story short, this is where the unlikely relationship between a twenty-six-year-old shop assistant and a seventeen-year-old youth began.

And, to begin with, despite Beattie's dominating personality, Sammy found this unlikely companionship to his liking, although his parents would have thoroughly disapproved had they known. For this reason, the affair was kept secret.

Inevitably, their relationship became more intimate. After the couple became lovers, Sammy would often excuse himself in the evenings, telling his mother that he was taking a walk down to the seafront for some fresh air, when in actual fact he was only nipping next door to see Beatrice in order to satisfy their mutual lust.

Eventually, these secret liaisons led to the inevitable; and, just four months later, Beattie announced to Sammy that she was pregnant.

Of course, when the news was passed on to Sammy's parents, they were naturally distraught.

"How could ye be sae silly?" his mother had wailed. "How could ye be tae'n in by a woman nearly ten years yer senior? How could ye no hae seen what she wis efter?

She's only gotten hersel' pregnant tae row ye in, the schemin' hussie!"

In order to preserve dignity, arrangements for the wedding were hurriedly put in place, and the couple were married without further delay. And it was on that day that Sammy could safely say that his life had definitely started to go downhill.

How he began to rue that hot afternoon during the summer of 1936 when he had accepted that cool glass of lemonade from his secret admirer in the flat upstairs.

With Beattie having sole occupancy of the residence above the Scotts, the obvious thing to do was to set up their matrimonial home in her flat. It was quite a simple and straightforward flit as far as Sammy was concerned; all he had to do was move himself and his few possessions upstairs!

And those few personal items were to be the only possessions that Sammy was ever going to be allowed to have, if Beatrice had her way, which of course she inevitably would.

From day one, Beatrice insisted that every penny Sammy earned was handed over. Now that she was a married woman, and soon to be a mother, Beattie had also decided that, in keeping with tradition, she would no longer have to keep on her job at the Co-op, leaving Sammy, with his pittance of a pay, as the sole breadwinner.

It was just as well that, with Beatrice having inherited the house from her parents as the sole beneficiary, there was no rent to pay.

After the food for the week had been bought, and the bills had been paid, any surplus was put away 'for a rainy day'. However, after the birth of their beautiful daughter, Alice, there was no more money to put away for that rainy day. In fact, the rainy day money rapidly became used up on essentials for the new baby.

"You'll have to look for another job", announced Beattie one morning. "What your father pays you is nowhere near enough to support us".

"But that's all he can afford to pay me", replied Sammy. "And he needs me. He couldn't possibly run the business these days without my help. He's not as fit as he used to be".

"Well, that's not our problem", she had replied condescendingly. "If he can't pay you a decent wage, then you'll have to look for work elsewhere".

Reluctantly, Sammy explained the situation to his father, then started to look for another job, with the promise that he would help out in the yard whenever he could find the time.

Deep within himself, however, he knew that any such arrangement would be at the discretion of his wife.

Eventually, he found work through the labour exchange as a street sweeper, or 'scaffie', as they were known locally, and was told to report to manager Mr. Tom McLeary at the local council yard on the following Monday morning.

"Ye look like a fine strong young man", remarked Mr. McLeary as he eyed Sammy up and down before pointing out where he should go to collect the tools of the trade, which consisted of a brush, a shovel, and a 'scaffie's barrie'; a contraption that looked like two galvanised dustbins attached to a wheeled frame.

"Do I not get any training for the job", Sammy had enquired.

"No, ye'll just hae tae pick it up as ye go along", his boss had answered with a chuckle. Unfortunately, Sammy was still too young and naive to appreciate such subtle humour.

As the days and months progressed, however, Sammy started to enjoy the work. It may have been a dirty and grimy job, but if the weather was fine it felt good to be out in the fresh air.

And the nine hours he was out of the house every day was nine hours away from his domineering wife.

It wasn't exactly a well paid job, but it was certainly better than what he had been earning from his father, and Beattie was once again able to put money away for that rainy day. Sammy, however, was never even allowed even so much as a penny for his pocket.

Life did have its blessings, though, and Sammy was totally devoted to his young daughter, who he loved more than anything else in the whole wide world.

Now aged one-and-a-half, little Alice was growing up fast, and she was the only thing that Sammy missed during the hours he had to spend away from the house. Without her, life would have been unbearable with just Beatrice to come home to every night.

Then, in September 1939, everyone's lives took a turn for the worse.

Listening to the radio in his parents' house (Beattie would not allow such an expensive commodity!); Sammy listened to that fearful announcement from Prime Minister Neville Chamberlain that the country "was now at war with Germany".

In the days that followed, an announcement was made that all men aged between twenty and twenty-three would, in all probability, be conscripted into the armed forces to fight for their country.

Sammy had only just entered into that age bracket. Probability then became inevitability and, before the end of the year, his call-up papers had dropped through the letterbox. He was to join the army.

Initially, he was filled with a sense of foreboding, fearful of what might lie in store.

However, after comforting himself with the common belief that 'it will all be over by Christmas', Sammy decided that he had no other option but to prepare himself to 'do his bit'.

And there was one further consolation. Although he would miss little Alice terribly, he would be away from the clutches of his dominating wife for the duration of the war!

The day that Sammy Scott went off to fight for his country duly arrived and, after bidding an emotional farewell to his infant daughter and giving Beattie a somewhat reluctant peck on the cheek, he made his way up to the railway station; where he, along with several other local conscripts, boarded the 10:57 and went off to war.

Sammy was perhaps more fortunate than the others when it came to being allocated their various regiments and duties. Whilst most found themselves enlisted in regiments that could well see man-to-man action on the front line, Sammy found himself part of a catering regiment, which was perhaps more suited to his rather shy and reserved nature.

Had he ever been in a situation where he may have had to kill another human being, it was doubtful if Sammy could have pulled the trigger.

That said, he would still be very much part of the war effort.

"An army can't march on an empty stomach", Sammy was constantly being reminded by his superiors.

Following some initial training, Sammy found himself over in France before the year was out, catering for the front-line soldiers that were employed building defences along the border with Belgium.

His time in the battle zone didn't last long, however, as he was evacuated from Dunkirk just a few months later when the British Army was forced to retreat from German advances.

After a period back in 'dear old blighty', during which he was able to return home for a very brief period of leave, Sammy was sent back overseas to resume his duties just behind the battle lines.

Throughout the remainder of the war, he served his country well, and his conduct had come in for the highest praise. He may not have been part of any hand to hand combat, but he had still been a vital part of the war effort, and the six years he had had to spend in uniform had made a man of him.

When he was finally released from the army, complete with his issue of demob clothing, which included a double-breasted pinstripe suit, shirts, shoes, a tie, a flat cap, and a raincoat, Sammy returned home in the mistaken belief that he would receive a hero's welcome from Beattie, and that things were about to change for the better.

When he walked through the door and stood before her, however, Beatrice just gazed at him before bursting out laughing at his ill-fitting clothes.

"You look ridiculous", she mocked. "They might have given you a suit that fitted! Mind you, it'll save the expense of having to kit you out in new clothes for a while."

Behind Beattie, looking rather shy and bewildered, stood Alice. Now nearly eight years old, she was rather unsure who this stranger was who had just walked into their house.

So much for the welcome Sammy that had expected from his wee girl, who he had thought would come bounding towards him with outstretched arms.

Eventually, life for Sammy returned to how it had been before the war. He was fortunate enough to get his scaffie's job back; but, just like in the days before he went off to fight for his country, every penny earned was handed over to Beatrice on pay day.

On a more positive note, however, Alice slowly grew to love her father, and eventually an inseparable bond grew between the pair. It was one of the few glimmers of light in an otherwise dull and mediocre existence.

Sammy's workmates were forever asking him if he fancied dropping in to the local for a pint after work, but this was, naturally, out of the question.

"Aye, his wife's no' the sort o' wummin ye'd tak hame a broken pay packet tae richt enough", observed one sympathetic colleague.

When works functions were organised, Sammy was always invited, but always declined, after having unsuccessfully sought Beattie's approval. In a very short time, he had earned himself the nickname 'Alaska'. This moniker had nothing to with having a cold personality; it was simply because, whenever such an invitation came along, he always replied: "I'll ask her"!

As the years passed, Sammy continued sweeping the streets, and living out his mundane life. Daughter Alice, who to all intents and purposes was his only reason for living, grew up to be a lovely, respectable young lady, who did exceptionally well with her education and, on leaving school, secured a good office job in one of the local factories. Like her father, however, she was required to hand over her pay packet every week to her domineering mother.

Then, one day, both Sammy and Alice's lives were to change forever.

Beatrice's health had been deteriorating steadily over the years, due mainly to the fact that she spent all day, every day, seated in her favourite armchair reading romantic novels and stuffing her face with the sort of luxuries she denied both her husband and daughter.

She was now grossly overweight, took absolutely no exercise whatsoever, and was basically a heart attack waiting to happen.

Arriving home from work one evening, Sammy found Beatrice slumped in the chair, her book in her lap, and a half-eaten box of chocolates scattered around the floor. She was stone cold dead.

Understandably, although shocked by her sudden death, both Sammy and Alice were not exactly overcome with grief at Beattie's sudden demise at the relatively young age of 56.

With Beatrice having no close relatives and few friends, the funeral was a small affair, attended by Sammy, Alice, and some of their colleagues, who thought it was perhaps only proper to show some sort of respect.

It was then Sammy's duty to sort out Beattie's estate, and he duly made an appointment with the bank manager to discuss the financial situation and have his late wife's bank account transferred into his name.

He wasn't in the least bit prepared for the shock that was in store. Never in a million years could he have foreseen the unbelievable piece of news that the bank manager was about to divulge. When Sammy heard what the manager had to say, you could have knocked him down with a feather.

Not only had Beattie been squirreling most of Sammy and Alice's income into her 'rainy day' savings account for several years, she had also been harbouring a secret for her entire married life.

As it turned out, Beattie's parents, when they had passed away over thirty years before, had left their daughter a substantial amount of money. A fortune that had been gathering interest ever since.

Although both Sammy and his daughter had never had any money to spend on themselves over the years, the family had been sitting on a fortune that was now worth well into five figures. They would never want for anything again!

It was now the 1960's, a decade when televisions, refrigerators and other such luxuries were commonplace in almost every home. These luxuries had never before been permitted in the Scott household, but that was all about to change.

Sammy wasted no time in kitting out their house with all the very latest 'mod cons', with the added luxury of being able to pay cash for every single item. Unlike most other households, nothing had to be bought 'on tick'.

This was the decade known as the 'Swinging Sixties', but Alice had never had the means to enjoy the latest pop music, not even so much as a transistor radio. Now she could afford the very best record player that money could buy.

Not only could she now afford to buy a brand new gramophone, she could also afford to buy all the latest chart hit records. Now, in the evenings, their little flat could be heard booming with the sounds of the hit parade. They could honestly say they had never been so happy.

For Sammy, Saturday nights were also to change forever. No more would he have to be entertained by reading the 'Sporting Post' over and over again (a rare luxury he was permitted on a Saturday evening), whilst Beattie lay slumped in her chair, having dozed off reading a chapter of her book.

From now on, Sammy would be spending Saturday nights supping a few pints accompanied by the odd nip 'chaser' down at the Boat Tavern!

It didn't take Sammy long to establish himself as a regular at the 'Boatie'; and, before long, he had come out of his shell and shaken off his shy nature.

He was a changed person, indulging in regular banter, and able to dish out as well as take a bit of good-natured ribbing when the opportunity arose.

It was several months later when, at closing time, Sammy just happened to leave the Boat Tavern slightly ahead of fellow regular Wullie Robb.

Walking a few paces behind Sammy, Wullie was puzzled when, just as Sammy passed the cemetery, he was seen to disappear through the bottom gate. Taking care not to be noticed, Wullie followed him into the graveyard, and looked on as Sammy made his way towards Beattie's grave.

Standing before the grave, Sammy took out his wallet, removed a wad of notes, bent over and waved them in front of the gravestone, before muttering:

"Aye, ye auld witch, try an' stop me spendin' yer money noo!".

Stifling a chuckle, Wullie waited until Sammy had exited the cemetery by the top gate, before making his way home.

Wullie couldn't wait to tell his chum, fellow Boatie regular Peter Thomson, about what he had just witnessed.

"Away", said Peter. "Ye're makin' it up!"

"I swear I am not", replied Wullie. "If ye don't believe me, we'll follow Sammy home this coming Saturday night at closing time and ye'll see for yourself!"

The following weekend, Sammy was at his usual place propping up the bar in the Boat Tavern; enjoying, as usual, a few beers and the company of the other regulars.

Last orders were duly called, Sammy drained the dregs from his glass, and bade farewell before making his way towards the door.

Wullie and Peter waited a few moments, before donning their coats and following on at a safe distance. Sure enough, Sammy made a detour through the cemetery, then performed his weekly ritual at Beattie's grave.

"Well, would ye credit it", uttered Peter. "I wouldn't have believed it if I hadnae seen it wi' ma ain eyes!"

"I have a plan", chuckled Wullie. "Next week we'll give Sammy a Saturday night to remember!"

The following week, Sammy, Wullie and Peter congregated as usual in the Boat Tavern, where they went through their usual ritual of downing a few pints, and having more than a few laughs. This week, however, both Wullie and Peter made their excuses just before last orders, and slipped out of the door.

Quickly, they made their way to the cemetery, where they concealed themselves behind Beattie's grave stone.

As sure as night follows day, Sammy appeared not long after ten o'clock, and went through his usual routine.

This time, however, when he leaned forward to wave the wad of notes in front of the gravestone, a hand appeared out of the darkness behind the stone and grabbed his wrist!

Sammy screamed and, still clutching the money, ran out of the graveyard as fast as his legs could carry him.

"She's maybe six foot under, but she's still tryin' tae tak' ma money aff me", he wailed as he hurriedly made his way home through the dark streets.

Wullie and Peter waited until Sammy was out of earshot, before both let out a guffaw of laughter.

"I dinnae think Sammy will ever visit his wife's grave on a dark Saturday night again", chuckled Wullie.

"Aye, and I think he'll need a fresh pair of underpants as soon as he's back in the hoose", added Peter.

The pair of wind-up merchants never told Sammy what they had done that night; and, as one would expect, Sammy never again made that detour through the cemetery on a Saturday after closing time!

5

Auld Alex

Sandy Smith reached up to the door bell, gave it a turn, and opened the front door.

"It's just me Mr. Fraser", shouted Sandy.

"Aye, come awa' through my wee man", shouted Alex.

Sandy walked up the lobby, opened the door of the living room, and cast his eyes over to where Auld Alex was seated in his favourite chair, next to his radio, which sat atop an old-fashioned sideboard. Alex offered his visitor a sweetie from the open bag that lay next to the radio, at the same time commenting "it's just a wee something tae taste yer mooth".

Sandy gratefully accepted the offer, and sat down on the settee that occupied the wall opposite the fireplace.

It was now almost a year since young Sandy Smith had started running errands for old Alex Fraser. Sandy was a keen member of the local cub pack; and, when it had been 'Bob a Job Week' during the school Easter holidays the previous April, Sandy had rung Alex's bell and asked if he needed a 'Bob a Jobber'.

Alex had been glad that Sandy had come to his door that day. Then in his seventy-fifth year, living alone and crippled with arthritis, Alex was not as mobile as he had once been, and he normally relied on his neighbours to get his messages in for him. His wife had passed away many years before, and his only other living relative, his daughter Helen, lived several miles away.

As he would normally have to stand at his door and wait for shop-bound neighbours to pass, he was glad that Sandy had saved him the trouble that day, and had sent the young lad to get some much-needed provisions from the local shops in return for the one shilling donation to the Cub Pack funds.

This was the 1960's. Few households even had fridges, never mind freezers and all the other modern conveniences that came to be taken for granted just a decade later.

Fresh meat or fish, milk, and other perishable goods, had to be purchased every other day, and stored in a cool cupboard. The bulk buying of food items to store in fridges and freezers simply couldn't be done in the sixties, and Auld Alex had looked upon young Sandy's offer of help as a Godsend.

When Sandy returned home at teatime that day, he told his mum all about Alex, and how he couldn't get out to do his messages because he was crippled.

"Well, that was nice of him to give you a shilling for running his errands", said his mother, before adding, "a shilling is a lot of money for someone like Alex, you know Sandy.
If you're passing his house in the future, maybe it would be a good idea to ring his bell and ask if he needs anything.
And if he tries to give you money, just refuse, and explain to him that part of the Cubs' Motto is to do a good turn for somebody every day".

And so it had begun. Auld Alex had been glad of the help; and young Sandy, as well as being proud to uphold the principles of the Cub movement, enjoyed the old man's friendship immensely, in particular his many tales of long ago.

He had a good way of relating a yarn, did Auld Alex. Sandy would sit enthralled, totally oblivious to the track of time, and on more than one occasion he had been late home for his tea as a result.

"Are ye needing any messages today?" asked Sandy.

"I would like a quarter-pound of mince from the butcher", replied Alex. "Now, make sure ye go tae Bob Beattie's. Dinnae go tae the ither one. I know he's closer, but I don't think his scales are accurate. I'm sure they're weighted in his favour. Now, could ye go through tae the scullery, hae a look in the press, and see if I have tatties and carrots?"

Sandy checked the cupboard. "Ye've tatties but nae carrots, Mr. Fraser".

"Well, ye'll need tae go tae the greengrocer as weel then. And seeing as ye're goin' there, ye might get me a quarter o' grapes. And whistle all the way back", added Alex with a glint in his eye, mildly implying that this would prevent Sandy from sampling a grape or two!

"I need bread from Simpson's as well", added Alex, as he handed Sandy five shillings. "Tell Lizzie who it's for, and she'll break a loaf in half. She knows I would never use a whole one, and there's plenty like me who'll gladly buy the other half".

Sandy took the money, grabbed Alex's string message bag from the scullery, and ran off down to Shore Street, where almost all of Seadykes' shops were situated.

"I'll go to the furthest away shop and work my way back", thought Sandy, as he dodged his way around the other shoppers.

"A quarter of mince please Mr. Beattie", he requested, looking up at the big, ruddy face of the butcher towering above him.

"Steak mince or beef mince?" asked Mr. Beattie.

"I'm not sure", replied Sandy. "It's for Auld Mr. Fraser".

"It'll be beef mince then", said the butcher, as he placed a lump of freshly ground meat on the scale, before adding a little more until the scale tipped over.

After wrapping it up, he handed the parcel down to Sandy, who then made his way over to the cashier's booth to pay for the goods.

Next stop was Simpson the baker, where as instructed he explained to Lizzie that he only wanted half a loaf.

"Aye, this'll be for Auld Alex", she remarked as she took a wrapped pan loaf and counted the slices inside the greaseproof paper before tearing it exactly through the middle. "How's he keeping these days? I haven't seen him in the shop for a while. Not since his daughter last visited, and took him out in his wheelchair".

"He's just the same as ever Mrs. Simpson", replied Sandy. "He says his arthritis is so bad some days he can't even rise off his chair".

"Ach, that's a shame", said Lizzie. "Well you tell him I was askin' after him".

"Aye, ah'll dae that", said Sandy as he took the bread before running out of the shop.

Next stop was the greengrocer, where Sandy had to wait his turn before Mr. Buchan served him with half-a-pound of carrots and a quarter of grapes.

"Is this for Mr. Fraser?", asked the greengrocer.

"Aye it is", replied Sandy.

Mr. Buchan winked and put some grapes in a separate bag.

"Ye're a good laddie runnin' messages for Auld Alex", said the greengrocer, "here's a few grapes for yersel!"

"Thanks Mr. Buchan, that means I'll no' have tae whistle on the way back", shouted Sandy as he left the shop; a remark that left the shopkeeper looking rather bemused!

Out of breath after having run all the way back to Auld Alex's house, Sandy pushed open the heavy front door and, after having deposited the messages in the scullery, made his way through to the living room and slumped down on the settee.

"Dinnae mak' yersel' comfortable just yet", said Alex. "It's time for oor cup o' tea, and ye know where the kettle is!"

Sandy sprang up, and ran through to the scullery, before filling the kettle at the sink. He then carefully turned on the gas and lit the flame using the battery-operated gas lighter, before placing the kettle on the ring.

Alex observed the youngster run back through to the living room and launch himself on to the settee.

"I wish I was still as agile as you, laddie", he said. "Unfortunately these days will never come again!"

"Never mind", replied Sandy. "You know you've got me".

This last comment almost brought a tear to Alex's eye. It was true. The old man really didn't know what he would do without young Sandy.

After a few minutes, the steam whistle on the spout of the kettle started to sound, before increasing pitch as the water inside started to reach boiling point.

Sandy stood up and made his way back through to the scullery, where he switched off the gas before lifting the teapot and two mugs down from the shelf.

Next, he got the tea caddy out of the cupboard. After he had, as instructed, warmed the pot by rinsing with some boiling water, he placed two teaspoons of tea in the pot and filled it up.

"Remember to let it mask for a few minutes now", shouted Alex.

"Aye, Mr. Fraser", replied Sandy, shaking his head. He had been making tea to Auld Alex's exact specifications for almost a year now, and surely by this time he knew the procedure!

After adding a dash of milk and two sugars to both mugs, Sandy carried the tea back through to the living room, where a grateful Alex blew fiercely on his before taking a long, noisy slurp.

"My, but ye mak' a fine cup o' tea, laddie", said the old man.

Sandy sat back up on the settee, mug in hand, and looked over at Alex. This was the part of his visit he loved the most, when he could get Mr. Fraser to tell him all about his adventures when he was a young man.

Sandy would sit in awe as Alex told him all about the places he had visited many years ago whilst working as a deck hand on various cargo ships. He claimed he had sailed all around the world, and had seen all the famous sights; like the Statue of Liberty and the SydneyHarbourBridge.

He also loved to be told about Alex's sporting prowess, when he had been one of the star footballers of his day, playing for several top teams in the Scottish League. The old man even claimed that he would have played for Scotland had he not picked up an injury just a week before he was due to make his debut against England at Hampden Park!

Sandy's favourite tale, however, was the story of how Alex had fought in the trenches during the First World War.

"Mr. Fraser, could you tell me again that story about when you were fighting in the war and you actually met a German soldier?" asked Sandy.

"Aye, your favourite story!", replied Alex. "Well, if you're sitting comfortably, I'll begin".

Sandy pulled over a cushion, placed it behind his head, and settled down.

"Well, as you know," started Alex, "this all happened a very long time ago, in the year 1916 to be precise. Our regiment had been sent over to France to fight against the Germans and, after several days of marching, we eventually set up camp near the River Somme.

A fierce battle between the Allies, which was the name given to the combined British and French armies, and the Germans, had started during the summer of 1916, and had been raging on with neither side making any progress.

Eventually, our battalion was told to take up position in the trenches that were positioned along the front. We knew that very soon we were going to be called into battle and try to advance towards the German lines."

"Weren't you frightened", asked Sandy.

"Oh, aye, we were all very frightened", replied Alex. "But you couldn't let anyone see you were scared. You just tried to be brave and pray to God that your life would be spared".

Sandy took a sip of tea, then sat back and listened as Alex resumed the tale.

"Anyway, the day after we took up position on the front line, we were told that we were to get ourselves prepared to go 'over the top'. We all sat and waited, terrified, as the sound of our artillery sent shells screaming into enemy territory. The idea of this was to disable the German guns before we went over, but it had little effect.
Then the sound of the whistle came. We all climbed up and over the trench wall, with bayonets attached to our rifles, and advanced towards the enemy lines. There were soldiers falling all around me as the German guns cut them down, but luckily I wasn't hit by a bullet during the early advance.

Then, a shell landed so close that I was blown off my feet and into a bomb crater.

I was knocked out by the blast, and when I eventually came round I was dazed and everything was blurred. Then, when my vision started to clear, I saw that there was someone else in the crater, a young German soldier. He was no more than a wee laddie".

"A wee laddie like me?" asked Sandy.

"Oh, he was older than you, my wee man", replied Alex. How old are you now?"

"I'll be eleven in three weeks time", replied Sandy.

"Well, in that case, he wisnae that much older!" remarked Alex.

"Ye see, young laddies lied about their age so that they could join the army and go off tae the war. They believed all the propaganda about how it was a glorious thing tae fight for King and Country, and they joined up without their Mum and Dad knowing".

"Really?" gasped Sandy. "They would be in big trouble!"

"Aye, they were in big trouble, but not just with their parents. The minimum age you had to be to become a soldier was eighteen, but a lot of young laddies much, much younger than that were recruited. The youngest soldier to fight at the Battle of the Somme, would you believe, was only twelve!"

"That's only about a year older than me!" remarked Sandy.

"Aye, and by all accounts the German army had soldiers of the same age. Anyway, I'll never forget the expression on his face. He was unarmed, having probably lost his rifle in the blast, and he was clearly terrified. He thought I was about to finish him off. But I just couldn't, could I? He was only a boy!

I did my best to calm him down, and tried to speak to him. I tried to find out which part of Germany he hailed from and how old he was.

Of course, because we spoke different languages, it was very difficult. But, by simply using a sort of primitive sign language, I was able to tell him that I was Alex, that I came from Scotland, and I was twenty-six years old.

The young German then pointed to himself and said "Hans, ich comme aus Hamburg", which I assumed meant his name was Hans and he hailed from the city of Hamburg. He then said "ich bin sechzehn" and showed me ten fingers, then six fingers, which must have meant he was only sixteen.

It was a very sobering moment. All the wartime propaganda that we had been fed throughout the conflict had claimed that we were going to war to fight an evil, villainous race. I now realised that the people we were being asked to kill were not dissimilar to ourselves, and they'd been forced to go to war under exactly the same circumstances that we had.

In all probability the Germans had been fed the same sort of propaganda that had been drummed into us, making them believe that it was the British who were the aggressors.

By this time the fighting was moving away from us. I looked at the young soldier, and motioned for him to stay silent as I started to climb up the side of the crater before making my way back to safety.

Just as I was about to take to my heels and run, the youngster caught hold of my trouser leg, and said "bitte, please", as he held out a good luck bracelet that he had been wearing around his wrist. He was so grateful that I had spared his life, he wanted to give me the bracelet as a token of thanks.

Realising that it would mean so much to the laddie if I accepted his gift, I grabbed it and put it in my pocket.

Well, to cut a long story short, I survived not only the Battle of the Somme, but the whole of the First World War, and maybe, just maybe, it was thanks to that good luck bracelet!"

"And you still have the bracelet to this day", broke in Sandy, knowing what was coming next, having heard the story several times before.

"Yes, I still have the bracelet", said Alex, as he opened a drawer in the sideboard and pulled it out.

Sandy gazed at the shiny bracelet in awe, before Alex returned it to the sideboard.

"Well, that's all for today", said Alex. Your mother will likely have your tea ready and be wondering where you are!

Sandy continued to be Alex's 'message laddie' for many a day. However, one afternoon, just over a year later, all that was to change rather suddenly.

As usual, Sandy rang Auld Alex's doorbell, opened the door, and shouted through to the living room, but there was no reply. A few moments later, a woman appeared at the living room door.

"You must be Sandy", said the woman.

"I'm Mr. Fraser's daughter, Helen. Could you come through to the living room for a minute please? There's something I have to tell you."

With a nervous feeling in his stomach that something was terribly wrong, Sandy followed the woman through. Casting his eyes around the room, there was no sign of Alex. His favourite chair beside the sideboard was empty.

"I'm awfully sorry to have to tell you", continued Helen, with a slight quiver in her voice, "that my Dad, Alex Fraser, passed away during the night".

Sandy sat down, dazed, on the settee.

"I would just like you to know, though, that Alex was very, very fond of you, and he really appreciated all that you did for him".

Tears started to well up in Sandy's eyes, and Helen handed him a tissue.

"Oh, I'm really going to miss him", wept Sandy. "I'm going to miss going for his errands; I'm going to miss our cups of tea; but most of all, I'm going to miss his stories".

"What sort of stories did he tell you?" enquired Helen.

"Oh, probably the same stories he would have told you when you were my age", replied Sandy.

"Stories like when he was a merchant seaman and sailed all around the world, seeing things like the SydneyHarbourBridge, the Egyptian Pyramids, the Statue of Liberty, and the Rock of Gibraltar. Then there was the story about when he played football and nearly got to play for Scotland. But the story I liked the best was when he fought in the war and spared the life of a young German soldier".

Helen frowned.

"But my Dad never went to sea, and he never played football. In fact, he couldn't run after a 'bus never mind run after a ball. And he certainly didn't fight in the war!

You see, my dad was a coal miner, and was exempt from being called up to fight in the armed forces. He spent the entire war the same way he spent his whole working life; hewing coal down the Wastby pits. He only moved to Seadykes when he retired. He thought the fresh sea air would be good for his lungs".

Sandy wiped his tearful eyes and stared at the woman in disbelief.

"But the German soldier gave him a good luck bracelet for sparing his life. It's in the drawer in the sideboard if ye dinnae believe me!"

Puzzled, Helen opened the drawer in the sideboard and pulled out the small trinket. She studied it before handing it over to Sandy.

Turning the charm over in his hands, Sandy had the opportunity, for the first time, to read what was on the back. He couldn't believe his eyes. What he had always been led to believe was a German good luck bracelet was actually inscribed:

MCPHERSON & SONS, JEWELLERS, GLASGOW.

Sandy stared at the object for a moment, then smiled. It looked like the old man had been pulling his leg all the time.

But Sandy didn't care. He was just grateful to have had Auld Alex for a friend, and he knew that the feeling had been mutual.

6

Comic Singer

"Well, you'll just hae tae play them at their ain game!" advised Wullie Robb as he propped up the bar at the Boat Tavern, surveying the near-empty hostelry.

"Aye, maybe you're right", replied mine host George Johnstone, as he stood behind the bar, polishing glasses with a dish cloth as he waited for one his meagre sprinkling of customers to order another pint.

It was Saturday night, and once again the pub was almost empty. Until recently, the 'Boatie' had been full to overflowing at weekends, from opening time right through to last-orders.

That had all changed when, at the other end of Shore Street, Seadykes' only other public house, the Sailor's Return, had started hosting live bands on Friday and Saturday nights.

It was the 1960's and, in the wake of 'Beatlemania', several bands from the cities were touring pubs and clubs in the smaller towns and villages all over Scotland, all seeking to make a name for themselves, as well as their fortune, by jumping on the pop music bandwagon.

"Who's playing at the Sailor's Return tonight?" enquired fellow Boatie regular Peter Thomson, as he wiped the froth from his lips on his coat sleeve.

"I believe it's a Glasgow band by the name of The Beatniks", replied George.

Apparently they've released a couple of singles this year and sold thousands of copies in their home city.

However, the story is that they've failed to make the charts because sales from Scottish record shops aren't taken into account when the national hit parade is being compiled".

"They seem tae hae a big enough following", commented barmaid Jeannie Smith, who was trying her very hardest to look busy behind the bar. "When I passed the Sailor's Return on my way here this evening there wis long queues waitin' tae get in!"

"Aye, that wid be oor main problem if we tried tae compete", lamented George. "They have a hall through the back of the pub with a stage. They could easily have about two hundred through there dancin' and enjoyin' the music. Mair tae the point, their tills will be ringin' all night when we're struggling to serve just a few beers to our regulars. Unfortunately, we've nae such facilities here".

"Could ye no' have just one singer, maybe wi' a guitar, sat on a stool in the corner?" enquired Wullie Robb. "It might be worth a try. There's maybe some local talent out there just waiting to be discovered!"

"Wullie could be richt, ye ken", piped in Jeannie. "Ye'll never know unless ye give it a go".

"Right, ye've made my mind up for me", announced George. "We'll advertise for solo performers, and set up an audition sometime through the week".

Meanwhile, sitting quietly in the corner, reading the day's football reports in the 'Sporting Post' was Boat Tavern regular Davie Wilson, who had been taking in every word of the conversation up at the bar.

Landlord George Johnstone's announcement had been music to Davie's ears, because ever since the distinctive 1960's pop music sounds had exploded on to the scene, Davie had held a secret notion to become a pop star himself.

Draining the dregs from his pint glass, Davie rolled up his newspaper and bade goodnight to his fellow regulars as he headed for the door. There was no time to lose.

"You're hame early", observed his mother as Davie entered the living room and handed her his 'Sporting Post'.

"Ach, the Boatie wis dead", replied Davie, "and anyway, I kent you wid be waiting on me bringing in the paper so that ye could try yer luck yet again in the 'Spot the Ball' competition".

"Will ye be wantin' a cup o' tea?" she enquired.

"Er, naw, I think I'll just hae an early night", replied Davie, before turning around and heading upstairs.

Once inside the safe sanctuary of his bedroom, he reached for his small transistor radio, and tuned it to Radio Luxembourg at 208 metres on the medium wave.

His plan, from now until the wee sma' hours of the morning, was to listen to the latest chart hits and write down the lyrics. All going well, he would before long have a repertoire of songs that couldn't fail to impress at the forthcoming audition!

True, he would also have to polish up on the few guitar chords he had learned whilst briefly a member of a local skiffle band during the 1950's.

Although the instrument had lain in his bedroom for ten years, and was badly in need of re-tuning, Davie was sure it would still be up to the job.

Pencil and notebook in hand, he strained his ears listening to the crackly tunes coming from the small inadequate radio speaker.

Although Radio Luxembourg played all the big hits of the day, it provided a somewhat unreliable service.

A combination of atmospheric conditions coupled with the hundreds of miles the radio signal had to travel from continental Europe meant that the reception kept drifting in and out. Davie was going to have to concentrate very hard in order to write down the lyrics correctly, and it was almost one in the morning before the would-be pop star finally closed his notebook. Job done!

From the many hits played that night, Davie had managed to successfully write down the words to three of them; one by American sensations The Monkees, who were at the time seriously challenging the Beatles for the hearts of the young teenagers on this side of the Atlantic.

Next was a popular number by the Rolling Stones that was sure to go down well. There were a lot of Stones fans in Seadykes, including Davie. Maybe, once he had managed to warm up his audience, he could encourage them to sing along with him? Davie's imagination was now starting to get a little carried away!

Last, but not least, was 'Release Me', the number one hit single by Englebert Humperdinck. Now that was sure to be a favourite with the ladies. Davie chuckled as he imagined some of the local women throwing skimpy underwear at him, just like they did at Tom Jones concerts!

Confident that the regular weekend spot at the Boat Tavern was as good as his, Davie drifted off to sleep dreaming of his future career as a pop idol. When word got out that there was a new star on the local pop scene, the 'Boatie' would surely be packed out all weekend.

The beer would be flowing, and a new generation of regulars would be singing along with Davie, who would be called back to do encore after encore as George Johnstone, behind the bar, frantically shouted "last orders please"; whilst Jeannie Smith did her best to serve one last drink to the multitudes of customers.

68

And surely they would have to take on extra bar staff? He would be the hero of the hour, having almost single-handedly saved his favourite 'local' from closure.

Of course, it would be no longer possible to walk the streets of Seadykes without having to weave his way through hordes of fans, all asking for his autograph.

And surely he would have to be paid handsomely once the Boat Tavern had become established as the top music venue in the local area! And would this new found wealth not afford him a flashy car and all the other luxuries that come with pop stardom?

Davie's dreams continued through the night, until he was rudely awakened late the following morning by the sound of his mother bawling up the stairs.

"Davie, ye'll have tae get up now or ye'll be late for the Kirk!"

That afternoon, once the weekly ritual of church attendance and its associated formalities were out of the way, Davie took advantage of the traditional day of rest to confine himself to his bedroom in order to polish up on his guitar playing and vocal skills.

For the first hour or so, his mother had griped about the noise emanating from his room, but when her protestations eventually ceased, Davie was certain that his playing and singing must have by then improved to the point where she no longer felt the need to complain.

In reality, she had been forced to go out for a walk to escape the din.

Over the days leading up to the audition, which had been set for Thursday afternoon, Davie went about his usual occupation as a lobster fisherman, but his mind was never far from this great opportunity that had been placed before him.

Once the creels had been hauled, their contents extracted, re-baited and thrown back into the water, Davie sang his heart out as he sailed back to the harbour.

The noise of the outboard motor, however, drowned out his singing to any other boats in close proximity, which was probably just as well.

When the big day finally arrived, Davie was beside himself with excitement. After having completed his usual routine during the morning, he headed home for a wash and a shave, and donned his best suit. It was important to make a good impression after all!

After a cup of tea and a quick sandwich, he grabbed his guitar and headed off down to the Boat Tavern. On entering the bar, he encountered Jeannie the barmaid, who was busily preparing the establishment for its five-o'clock opening.

"Hiya Jeannie", he said, with a little nervousness creeping into his voice. "I'm here for the audition!"

Jeannie looked Davie up and down.

"Well I never! Davie Wilson! I never knew you could sing never mind play the guitar! You'd better go through to the lounge, where the other hopefuls are all seated awaiting their call through to the audition. George will be here soon to hear what you all have to offer, and he's asked me to assist him select the best act".

This was music to Davie's ears. He knew landlord George Johnstone well enough, but he knew Jeannie had a soft spot for him, and having her on the panel was surely going to be to his advantage!

Davie gingerly opened the door of the 'Snug', and took a seat. Looking around, he saw that there were three other candidates for the job.

To his right was a guy with a guitar who was wearing a black leather jacket with the collar turned up. His thick black hair was swept back in a huge wave, and it looked like his big bushy sideburns had been stuck on with glue.

To his left sat a girl with long black hair, who for some reason was wearing no shoes; and to her left was a girl with red hair.

The red head was chatting away to the girl with no shoes and was trying hard to sound like she had a Liverpool accent, but it was patently obvious she hailed from one of the neighbouring fishing villages.

"Hiya, I'm Davie Wilson", he announced.

"Pleased tae meet ya, chook!", said the red headed girl.

"Powerful glad to make your acquaintance", said the guy in the leather jacket, who was making a poor job of trying to sound like he had been born and brought up in Tupelo, Mississippi.

The girl with no shoes simply looked over and smiled.

After sitting for what seemed like an eternity, mine host George Johnstone poked his head around the door. When his eyes fell on Davie Wilson, his heart sank. This wasn't exactly the sort of local talent he had in mind. Hopefully the other candidates wouldn't be as gormless!

"Right, we're ready for the first singer" he announced. "Would you like to come through to the bar?" he asked the red head.

The girl stood up and made her way through. Moments later, the air was filled with the sound of the pub's piano accompanying the red-headed girl's rendition of 'Anyone Who Had a Heart'; the recent number-one hit for Cilla Black.

"Aye, no' bad", thought Davie. "But the piano could dae wi' a tune".

Next up was the guy with the leather jacket; who, almost as soon as the door was closed, burst into:

"Ah well it's one for the money; two furr the show; three tae get ready; noo go, cat co; but don't you, step on mah blue suede shoes . . . . ."

Davie looked over at the girl with no shoes.

"Aye, he's no bad either. I think we'll baith hae a job tae beat thae twa'!"

The girl smiled back sweetly, before replying:

"It's all the hanging around I don't like. You wait, you wait and wait".

After what seemed like an age, the dulcet tones of the Elvis impersonator faded away, and the girl with no shoes was called through.

Before long, the sound of Sandie Shaw's 'Always Something There To Remind Me' filled the air; but, unlike the first two candidates, this singer had neither guitar nor piano to accompany her.

"Maybe, just maybe", thought Davie, "if she gets the job and I dinnae, I could offer tae be her guitarist!"

At long last it was Davie's turn for the audition. Standing before George and Jeannie, he tried to look professional by adjusting the microphone and tapping the end of it, before saying: "one two; one two".

"Right, let's get on wi' it" said George. "What song do you have for us".

"I've actually got three songs for you", replied Davie.

George and Jeannie exchanged glances, before Jeannie sighed and said "okay, then. If ye must!"

Davie cleared his throat.

"The first number ah'mm goin' tae sing fur ye is by The Monkees", announced Davie, trying to sound as professional as he could, "and it goes like this:"

Accompanied by his questionable guitar playing, Davie then burst into song, and all went well for the first few lines.

"I thought love was only true in fairy tales,

Meant for someone else but not for me;

Ah, love was out to get me,

That's the way it seemed,

Disappointment haunted all my dreams"

"Actually", Jeannie thought to herself, "that would be just about passable if the guitar playing was polished up a bit". Jeannie, however, was just about to eat her words, as Davie launched into the chorus:

"But then I saw her face, now ah'mm gonna leave her,

No not a trace of doubt in my mind;

And those lugs? Oh, no, ah'mm gonna leave her,

Ah'mm Gonna leave her, bye bye".

George and Jeannie looked at each other in disbelief, then George turned to Davie.

"Where did you get the lyrics from?" he asked. "They're, em, shall we say, not quite right?"

"Oh, I listened to the songs on Radio Luxembourg and wrote the words down as I heard them", replied Davie.

"Right, okay, that figures", said Jeannie. "The radio signal can drift in and out, and you've obviously just misheard that one. Nothing that can't be fixed though, I suppose. Right then, let's hear your next song".

Davie composed himself, and tried again to look and sound the part.

"The next number ah'mm gonna do is by the Rollin' Stones", he announced. "It's the one about the shopkeeper trying to break up a fight. It's called 'Get Off MacLeod'."

"I think you'll find the song is actually called "Get Off My Cloud", said George, "and I didn't realise it was about someone trying to stop a fight!"

"Aye, that's what I said", replied Davie. "Get Off MacLeod".

Jeannie sighed. "Right then. Whatever you say. Just get on wi' it please".

After a poor attempt at trying to master the guitar intro, Davie burst into song:

"I live in an apartment on the floor above my shop,
And looking out the window I thought the world had stopped,
Then in flies these guys, and I see it's you and Jack,
And next thing I know you've jumped up on his back.

I said hey, Hughes, get off of MacLeod,
Hey, Hughes, get off of MacLeod,
Hey, Hughes, get off of MacLeod,
Runnin' around all through the town".

"Davie, Davie, Davie", Jeannie screamed, trying to make herself heard above the racket. "Stop! Stop! You've got the words entirely wrong! Look, I really don't think you're the guy for this job".

"Oh please!" replied Davie. "Ah can dae this. PLEASE gie me wan mair chance. Will ye let me sing ma final song?"

George sighed before glancing at Jeannie, and then said "right, one last chance".

"For mah final number", announced Davie, "ah'mm gonna sing 'Release Me' that number wan hit by Englebert Humperdinck".

"At least he's got the title right this time", thought Jeannie.

Davie launched into his final number, determined to give it his very best shot and, after a questionable guitar intro, burst forth with:

"The police released me, let me go,

Now I don't rob you anymore,

I didnae like tae be locked in,

But they released me, and I'll no' rob again.

I have found a new career,

And I will always . . . ."

"Davie! Stop!" Jeannie screamed.

George shook his head then stared at the ceiling; whilst Jeannie slumped down in the chair with her head in her hands.

"So ye've heard enough tae make up yer minds?" asked Davie.

"Aye", said George.

"And am I in wi' a chance then?"

Jeannie and George exchanged glances, before Jeannie sighed and said:

"Er, Davie . . look, er. . we'll umm, we'll let you know".

7

An Unlikely Hero

The lifeboat is a vital part of any fishing community. Fisher folk, since time immemorial, have always felt a duty to protect and save the lives of their fellow seafarers.

It is their belief, and rightly so, that they could one day be the ones in peril on the sea, and feel it is their duty to volunteer to be part of such a service.

The coastal fishing town of Seadykes is no exception.

A lifeboat station was first established in the town in the mid-nineteenth century, just a few years after the RNLI, The Royal National Lifeboat Institution, had been founded.

Ever since then, the station and lifeboat has been manned by local volunteers; and, as the service became developed over the years, it has attracted volunteers from all walks of life, not just from the local seafaring community.

Since its inception, the Seadykes lifeboat has taken part in several rescues, and hundreds of lives have been saved. The lifeboat crews have been called from their beds in all sorts of weather at a moment's notice; they have hurriedly dressed and raced down to the lifeboat station; and have then put out to sea, risking their own lives to save the lives of others.

They are heroes, every one.

However, there are also those lifeboat volunteers who are rarely seen in the limelight, but who are still a vital part of the operation.

They are the people behind the scenes; the volunteers who carry out vitally important duties; and one of the most important of these duties is that of the lifeboat launcher.

And of all the launchers who had volunteered their services to the Seadykes lifeboat over the years, their most loyal servant of all was, in all probability, Archie Watson.

Archie had initially joined the lifeboat service with a view to becoming a crew member. However, despite his undoubted willingness to put his life at risk for the sake of others, he was turned down on the grounds of having a vision impairment, colour blindness to be precise, which had been diagnosed during his medical.

Archie was still determined to be involved, however, and when he was then offered a position as a launcher, he jumped at the chance.

That was over ten years ago now, and in those years Archie had helped launch the lifeboat on numerous occasions. In doing so, he had played his part in saving many lives. If the lifeboat couldn't be put to sea, after all, there was no way the crew could go to the assistance of anyone!

There had been many memorable rescues carried out during Archie's time at the lifeboat shed. The first major one he had been involved in was when the Johanna Bergmann, a German collier bound for Hamburg, had grounded on the rocks off the neighbouring fishing village of Toreness during a fierce storm in the early 1950s.

It had proved impossible to set up a breeches buoy (a rope device) from the Toreness shore to rescue the crew; and, as the use of helicopters for air-sea rescue had yet to be introduced, the only way the crew of ten could be brought to safety was to set up a breeches buoy between the lifeboat and the ship, an extremely perilous operation!

The rescue had taken several hours, and when the lifeboat eventually made it back safely to Seadykes harbour, Archie had been on hand to help the cold, wet and exhausted German seamen off the lifeboat before escorting them to the shed, where their recovery was assisted with a cup of hot cocoa and a warm blanket.

Then there was the time when a plane from the nearby R.A.F. base had been forced to ditch in the sea several miles from shore. It had been a filthy night; and the lifeboat, which had been launched just after ten-o'clock in the evening, did not return until dawn.

After having searched all through the night, scanning the sea with a powerful search lamp, the crew eventually managed to locate and rescue the two airmen, who were suffering from exposure after having been tossed around in their small life raft for several hours.

These incidents, and more, had been regularly reported in the press, and Archie took the greatest delight in cutting out the newspaper reports and pasting them in a scrap book.

Not that he would want any of the lifeboat staff to know that he kept such a record; he just thought that some day in the future it might be good to look back on the rescues that he had taken part in, albeit just as one of the shore crew.

There was to be one cutting, however, that was destined to take pride of place in Archie's scrap book.

That particular story had started to unfold on a gorgeously sunny and hot Sunday afternoon in early July. In those far-off days of the 1960's, the residents of Seadykes, and, for that matter, almost every other fishing community in Scotland, still respected 'The Lord's Day'.

Only leisure activities were indulged in and, apart from those people who provided vital services, working on a Sunday was simply unheard of.

Almost every family had been to church that morning and, after having enjoyed Sunday lunch with extended family members, as was the tradition, most had decided to take full advantage of the pleasant cloudless afternoon.

Most of the lifeboat crew had either gone to the local beach with their families, or were relaxing and enjoying a swim at the Seadykes open air swimming pool.

Archie was enjoying the latter. He had always been a strong swimmer, having braced the chilly seawater-filled pool for a 'dook' ever since he had been a young laddie, as had most of his school chums.

Then, all of a sudden, the weather changed. There had hardly been a breath of wind all day; then, without warning, the skies clouded over, and a sudden squall coupled with a deluge of rain sent the picnickers, sunbathers and swimmers scurrying for shelter.

The precipitous change in conditions was also causing problems far out to sea, where a small yacht, with two young and inexperienced crew members on board, had been caught unawares.

They had been progressing across the estuary in full sail when the unforeseen change in weather conditions had caught them out, almost causing the small craft to capsize. In doing so, the vessel had taken on a lot of water; and, although it had subsequently returned to an upright position, its rigging had been damaged to the extent that it was rendered useless.

As the yacht had no auxiliary back-up engine, it was now drifting helplessly, being tossed around in the choppy sea, and the crew was in grave danger.

It was extremely fortuitous that the yachtsmen had taken the precaution of including flares in the vessel's itinerary, or their predicament could have been even more severe.

They were also fortunate that their distress signal had been observed by the local coastguard station, who had consequently arranged for the lifeboat rockets to be launched in order to alert the lifeboat crew.

It was when the rain-soaked sun-seekers were heading for home that the ear-shattering sound of the lifeboat rockets echoed through the streets of Seadykes.

As they were conditioned to do, everyone associated with the lifeboat station immediately set off for the harbour by whatever means would take them there the quickest.

Being a Sunday, there was a full complement of volunteers to choose from, and coxswain Hamish Cattenach had no difficulty in selecting his crew, with helmsman Duncan Allanson and mechanic Gordon Baird receiving the nod along with additional crew members Dougie Bruce and Malky Jamieson.

The five men quickly donned their waterproof oilskin suits and put on their lifejackets before taking up position on the lifeboat.

The rescue craft then slid down the slipway that led from the shed into the harbour; and, once it the water, the boat started to motor towards the harbour mouth, where it started to accelerate before heading out at full power into the open sea.

The flat-calm conditions that had existed earlier in the day had now given way to a much choppier sea, with white crests topping the four-foot waves.

Coxswain Hamish Cattenach set the course of the lifeboat towards the position indicated by the coastguard, and they forced their way in the direction of the stricken vessel through the worsening conditions.

About half-an-hour later they arrived at the yacht's last known position, but there was no sign of the sailboat.

With winds now reaching gale-force, it was almost certain that the small craft had drifted several miles away, so the coxswain ordered the lifeboat to proceed in the direction the wind might have carried it, with all hands scanning the horizon as they went.

Visibility was by this time very poor, and the lifeboat crew was finding it increasingly difficult to see for any distance. The waves were now reaching five to six feet in height, which was also hampering the search.

Despite the conditions, and despite the fact that the crew members on the open and exposed deck were starting to feel the effects of the cold, the search went on unabated.

Meanwhile, back at the lifeboat shed, Archie and the other launchers were kept up to date on the situation by the coastguard station, who were in constant radio contact with the rescue party. It soon became apparent that they might have a long wait before the lifeboat returned.

Back out at sea, the search continued. Then, just as the lifeboat was lifted up by a rising wave, Malky Jamieson thought, just for a split second, that he had spotted something in the distance.

"Over there, a mast!" he shouted, pointing to the south east.

Coxswain Hamish Cattenach lifted his binoculars and focussed on the point that Malky had indicated.

"How far away?" he shouted.

"About half-a-mile"

With the lifeboat constantly rising to the crests of the waves before immediately falling back into the troughs, any sighting of a vessel in distress was only going to be for a split second.

Hamish continued to scan the horizon as best as he could.

"I cannae see anything, Malky. Are you sure?"

"As sure as I can be with the boat rising and falling like it is", came the reply. "Right, let's head over in that direction" shouted Hamish. "Malky, you guide us".

As the lifeboat headed in the direction of the sighting, Malky started to doubt himself. There had just been that one glimpse. What if he had been wrong? What if his tired eyes had simply been playing tricks?

However, just as he was about to give up and admit to the coxswain that he might have been mistaken, came a shout from Dougie Bruce, who was keeping an eye out to the north-east.

"There it is, over there" he yelled, holding his arm up and pointing.

The rest of the crew peered into the distance.

"Aye, there she is! There's the yacht over there!" shouted Duncan Allanson, scanning the horizon as he steered the boat.

Hamish Cattenach focussed his binoculars where Dougie and Duncan had indicated. Sure enough, there it was. A small yacht, no more than eighteen feet long, being tossed around in the raging sea with its sails ripped to shreds.

"You're right enough lads, well spotted! Let's get over there and get these poor lads to safety".

As the stricken vessel was still being carried away in the gale-force wind, the lifeboat had to increase its speed to the maximum that the conditions would allow, but it still took over half-an-hour before they managed to catch up with the yacht. Through the windows in the side of the cabin, they could just make out two figures.

However, the crew were then faced with a further dilemma.

Should they attempt to get alongside the drifting yacht and somehow transfer the tired, weary and frightened yachtsmen to the lifeboat, leaving their vessel to its fate?

Or should they attempt to get a member of the lifeboat crew on to the yacht, where a rope could be then be attached in order to take the vessel in tow?

A decision had to be taken quickly, and it was decided that the safest solution would be for one of the lifeboat crew to board the yacht.

"Any volunteers?" asked coxswain Hamish.

"I'll do it" replied Dougie Bruce, quick as a flash. "I'm the strongest swimmer here, and there's every chance that whoever tries to get aboard will end up in the sea".

"Good lad" shouted Hamish. "Get yourself ready to jump".

Skilfully, helmsman Duncan Allanson steered the lifeboat alongside the yacht. Dougie, after waiting for a wave to lift the adjacent craft to a suitable level, launched himself over the gap and on to the deck of the yacht.

After grabbing on to the mast in order to steady himself, he made his way aft, keeping a tight hold of the rail, before entering the yacht's saloon through a door in the rear cockpit.

Inside, he found two ashen-faced young lads of around eighteen years in age, who looked terrified to say the least.

"Boy, are we glad to see you", said the one nearest to Dougie through chattering teeth.

"And boy were we glad tae find ye!" replied Dougie.

"Right, here's the plan. I'm going back up on to the deck, where hopefully I'm going to catch a rope thrown from the lifeboat. I'll attach it to the bow of your craft, then we're going to attempt to tow you back to the harbour. I want you to stay in here and try to stay calm and keep warm as best as you can".

"Don't worry", replied the other lad. "There's no way we're going back out there!"

After several missed attempts, the tow rope was finally secured, and the two vessels started their long and arduous journey back to Seadykes harbour.

The news of the rescue was relayed back to the shed, where Archie was advised to prepare for the return of the boat later that evening.

It was going to be another couple of hours at least before the lifeboat crew, and those they had rescued, were back on dry land and the lifeboat back in its shed.

Back inside the yacht's saloon, Dougie started chatting to the two lads; partly to find out what had happened, but mainly because they were cold and wet and there was a possibility of hypothermia setting in. Under circumstances such as these, the victims could well fall unconscious, and it was best to keep them talking.

Fortunately, although dressed in light summer clothing, both had had the good sense to put on their wrap-around lifejackets. As well as being a vital buoyancy aid, the jackets provided an additional layer of warmth, which in itself could prove to be a lifesaver.

It was now just before seven o'clock in the evening. Although the lifeboat was now heading into the wind, and had the yacht in tow, there was a good chance they would be back in the harbour before darkness fell.

Dougie tried his best to keep the teenagers amused.

Meanwhile, on board the lifeboat, the remaining crew members huddled together in the small shelter beside the engine room in an attempt to keep out the chill. Despite the fact that it was mid-summer, the open sea could still be a bitterly cold place!

Eventually, at quarter-past-nine, the two vessels were finally approaching the safety of the harbour. The wind had now dropped and the rain had ceased; and, with word having got around that a dramatic rescue had taken place, a sizeable crowd had gathered at the end of the main pier.

In that crowd was a photographer from a national newspaper, who had been in the local area covering an unconnected event, and had been tipped off about this possible news story whilst making his way back west.

When the lifeboat finally entered the harbour, it became apparent that the crew were now facing another, very different, problem.

The tide had gone out, and it was therefore not possible to manoeuvre the lifeboat up to the slipway to allow it to be hauled up into the shed. The crew had no other option but to berth the lifeboat, with the yacht alongside, in the only water that still remained in the harbour at low tide, directly below the waiting crowd!

Archie Watson, along with the other launchers, had waited patiently in the lifeboat station all afternoon and into the evening; but as the time had progressed and the tide had receded, he and his fellow volunteers realised that they wouldn't be able to get the boat back into the shed that night.

Instead, they would be required to assist with securing the lifeboat in its temporary berth, and they had duly made their way to the end of the pier to await its arrival, where they had to fight their way through the company of onlookers to take up their respective positions.

When the two craft came alongside, Archie threw down a rope, which Malky Jamieson secured to the bow of the lifeboat. Mechanic Gordon Baird, who had now emerged from the engine room, secured another rope to the stern.

After the vessel had been secured fast to the bollards on the pier, Archie climbed down a stepladder and onto the lifeboat, before making his way over to assist with securing the yacht to the other side of the vessel.

Once this was done, it was time to transfer the cold and tired yachtsmen to the safety of dry land, and to do this the men had to perform the relatively simple task of stepping from one boat to the other before climbing up on to the pier.

However, just as the first weary sailor was stepping across the gap between the yacht and the lifeboat, he suddenly lost his footing and plunged into the cold water of the harbour. The young lad wasn't a good swimmer; and, despite having a lifejacket to keep him afloat, he panicked and waved his arms around, causing the water to splash up all around as he did so.

Quick as a flash, Archie lay down on the deck and reached out to grab the unfortunate seafarer. Grabbing him by the arm, he managed to calm the yachtsman down, before Duncan Allanson came to Archie's assistance, and the young man was pulled to safety.

This minor incident was all over in a matter of seconds. However, the ever-alert press photographer hidden amongst the spectators on the pier had been in the right place at the right time.

Oblivious to Archie and the rest of the lifeboat crew, he had captured the very moment that a hand had been offered to the guy who had fallen into the water.

Having got what he came for, the paparazzo put his camera back in its case, pulled up the collar on his raincoat, and quickly made his exit.

There was no time to lose if he wanted to beat the deadline for the following morning's paper!

Meanwhile, the yachtsmen were safely transferred to the pier, and the vessels were made secure. The tired lifeboat crew and launchers then proceeded to make their way home, safe in the knowledge that they had, once again, come to the aid of mariners in distress.

They had, in all probability, saved the lives of the two young and inexperienced sailors.

The following morning, Archie rose early and made his way down to the harbour. The tide was now back in, and the lifeboat could finally be returned to the shed.

Waiting for him was coxswain Hamish Cattenach, along with mechanic Dougie Bruce and another couple of volunteers.

"Here he comes, the hero of the hour!" declared Hamish.

"Aye, behold the saviour of the drowning sailor", declared Dougie, with just a hint of sarcasm.

Archie looked at them and frowned.

"What are ye talkin' aboot lads?" he asked, with a genuine look of puzzlement.

"Come on now, dinnae be sae modest. Ye're bound tae hae seen the front pages this mornin'! Yer photie's splashed a' ower the national press!" said Dougie with a smirk.

"I genuinely have nae idea whit ye're goin' on aboot" replied Archie. "Why wid my photie be in the paper?"

"Here, tak' a look" said Hamish as he pulled that morning's edition of the 'City Press' out from beneath his jacket.

There, to Archie's disbelief, he found himself staring at a full page photo of himself, lying on the deck of the lifeboat and reaching down to grab the arm of the yachtsman who had fallen into the harbour.

However, the picture had been altered in order to cut out the background; which, along with the splashing caused by the panicking sailor, it look as if the incident had occurred far out to sea.

To anyone not familiar with the actual circumstances under which the photo had been taken, it looked very much as if Archie had reached out just in time to save the unfortunate man, who was about to lose his battle to stay afloat.

Casting his eyes to the top of the page, Archie read the headline:

PLUCKED
FROM
THE
TEMPEST

Beginning to flush with acute embarrassment, he then looked at the bottom of the page, where the sub-headline read:

SEADYKES LIFEBOAT CREWMAN SAVES SAILOR FROM CERTAIN DROWNING!

Shaking his head in disbelief, Archie folded the newspaper and handed it back to Hamish.

"Look, guys, ah'm really sorry. You're the real heroes, not me. I really dinnae know whit tae say".

"Say nothing, and enjoy the moment", chuckled Hamish. "We all know its just journalistic licence. We all know that the newspapers just twist the facts around in order to sensationalise news stories".

"And anyway", cut in Dougie. "It's aboot time ye got some sort of acknowledgement for yer devotion tae duty ower the years".

Archie smiled to himself. He really wasn't looking for any sort of recognition. Just to be part of a life-saving organisation was enough reward as far as he was concerned. Having said that, however, that front page was about to take pride of place in his scrap book!

8

The Haver

"Brace yourselves, here he comes", announced Jackie Campbell, as she looked up from her desk and over at the approaching figure who could be seen through the glass panel of the office door.

"Oh, spare us!" sighed Jackie's colleague Rab Stewart, who put down his pencil, raised his arms, and put his hands behind his head, preparing himself for Jimmy Walker's latest far-fetched tale.

A "haver", in old Scots parlance, is someone who has a reputation for, shall we say, being rather economical with the truth when relating a tale to a weary and brow-beaten audience. Jimmy Walker fitted that description perfectly.

To say that Jimmy exaggerated the point was an understatement. It was perhaps more fitting to say that his stories were pure fiction with a smattering of truth added in a vain attempt to make the tale believable!

Now in his late fifties, Jimmy Walker had been employed as a delivery driver for Seadykes Seafoods for over twenty years and, during that time, must have told hundreds, if not thousands, of far-fetched tales.

Rab and Jackie, who worked in the company's office, had long-since learned that it was best just to keep quiet and listen patiently to Jimmy's fables. To interrupt and cast doubt on the validity of his yarns would simply have resulted in an even more ridiculous account of whatever he was 'havering on about' on that particular day.

It was Monday morning and, with Jimmy having only just returned from his summer holiday in the south of England, both Jackie and Rab knew that they were in for a long, drawn out series of implausible stories. And, to make matters worse, it could sometimes be hard to understand what Jimmy was saying, as his vernacular was, shall we say, rather difficult to comprehend.

In addition, both Rab and Jackie suspected that Jimmy occasionally made up words of his own. In fact, Jackie had even suggested that they write down these seemingly fabricated words for future reference in the form of a tongue-in-cheek 'Walker Dictionary'.

"Well, how was the holiday?" enquired Rab, knowing full well that he was inevitably going to hear all about it anyway, and it was perhaps best if he got the ordeal over with sooner rather than later.

"Weel, ah'll tellye, it wis bilin'!" replied Jimmy.

"So you're saying it was very hot then?", enquired Jackie, after having managed to decipher what Jimmy had just said.

"Aye. It wis bilin', an' jistisweel tha ho-ell hid a pool tae coolaffin".

"Oh, the hotel had a pool? That must have been nice!" said Jackie.

"Aye, bittitwis sae hoat thit twa' fittowatter evapperraetit ootoad in wan efternane!".

"Really? It must have been hot for two feet of water to be lost from the pool through evaporation!" commented Rab.

"Ye see, we wis tellt thur wis a heat wave cummin. An' whan it arrived fowk startit screamin an' rinnin fir sheltir. Some jumpit in the pool, bit the wattir wis that bilin' they wis lucky they wisnae turn'd tae soup!"

It was patently obvious that Jimmy had no idea what a heat wave actually was.

"How high did the temperature go?" enquired Jackie, knowing full well that the answer would very probably far exceed the official British record.

"Weel", replied Jimmy, "thurwissa thurmommitur aside the pool. An' we wis lookin' at it an' it wis gaunupannup, an it got tae ninety-fower degrees".

"Ninety four degrees Fahrenheit? That was certainly hot!" observed Rab.

"Fahrenheit? Naw, Centigrade!" Jimmy retorted.

Rab and Jackie tried not to laugh as they exchanged glances. They knew that, no matter how ridiculous the tale, it was best just to keep their mouths shut. But it was difficult.

"Well, I'm sure you're glad to be home then, an' ye'll be keen to get back out on yer deliveries", said Rab, as he tried to bring a hasty end to that particular morning's havering.

"Aye, ah hid bettir be gettinon", replied Jimmy, before adding "ah'll tell ye's mairabootit anither time".

"Aye, I'm sure ye will", sighed Rab. "Me an' Jackie'll look forward tae that!"

Jimmy the Haver left the office and embarked on his daily duties, no doubt relating to every customer on his rounds the epic tale of his eventful week in the searing heat.

And, true to his word, every finite exaggerated detail of his journey to the south of England was related throughout the week to Rab and Jackie, who tried their very best to maintain poker faces.

At long last, the weekend arrived.

At finishing time on the Friday, Jackie bumped into Jimmy as he was clocking off.

"Well, what are you up to this weekend?" enquired Jackie.

"Ah'm gowfin'", replied Jimmy. "An' ahm hopin' tae gitta holinwann like ahdiddafore", he proudly predicted.

"A hole in one!" remarked Jackie. "You must be a good golfer".

"Oh, aye" replied Jimmy. "Thurs no monny kin haudacaunle tae me doon at the gowf club. Ah'll drap in efter tha weekend an' let ye kin hooah gotton".

"Yes, I'm sure you will", sighed Jackie. "I'm sure you will".

Sure enough, after an all-too-short weekend, Jimmy came breezing through the office door on Monday morning to relate his latest improbable tale from the golf course.

"No' wan bit twa', annah got roond in suxty-wan!" he announced as he made his way across the office floor.

"How do you mean?" asked Rab.

"Twa' holesinwann", replied Jimmy. "An ah feeneeshed aleeven unner par".

"Two aces and eleven under par? That must be something of a club record!"

"Aye, ah keep brekkinem" declared Jimmy. "An noo ra high heid yins ittra gowf club are spikkin aboot makin' me tee aff wi' a saund irn instead o' a drevver tae gie obbdy else a chaunce!"

Rab tried hard to keep his face straight.

"Jimmy, just to make sure we're not talking at cross purposes, are you seriously trying to tell us that, because you keep breaking club records, the officials at the golf course now want you to tee off using a sand iron?"

"Aye, tae begeen wi", replied Jimmy, "that's whit thur gonntae mak me dae. Afore lang, though, they reckon ah'll hae tae gan roon' the hale coorse wi' jist a saund irn."

Jackie, in an attempt to stifle a guffaw, exhaled sharply down her nose and, in doing so, made the strangest of noises.

"Whitts rang wi' you?" enquired Jimmy.

"It was just a sneeze", lied Jackie. "I think I must have a cold coming on".

"Weel, time tae get oot on ma roonds afore ah catch the smit", announced Jimmy as he covered his nose with his hand, and off he went.

The days, weeks and months passed, and the dubious stories continued unabated. Summer gave way to autumn; winter set in all-too-soon, then spring eventually arrived, throughout all of which Jimmy the Haver related his tales to anyone who would listen.

Or, more to the point, anyone who hadn't seen Jimmy approaching.

Then, one morning in early April, Jimmy burst into the office in a state of excitement.

"Hae ye heard? Wastby Wanderers hiv made it shroo taerah final. Thuh've bate the Roavurrs in last nicht's replay, an' thur tae play Castleburgh attra nashnall staydyium furrahcup in a foartnicht's time."

"Aye, we heard", replied Rab.

In fact, last night's match had been the only topic of discussion in the office that morning ever since the staff had clocked on an hour earlier.

Although the mining conurbation of Wastby lay several miles to the west, Wastby Wanderers had always been thought of as the local senior team, and a fair contingent of the club's regular supporters came from Seadykes and the neighbouring villages of Toreness and St. Dronans.

For the Wanderers, a provincial club, to have made it through to the cup final was indeed a remarkable achievement!

"Hoozaboot", enquired Jimmy, "wuh see wha's eentristit in gaun taerah final, an' mabee git Tam Broon tae tak' us through innis meenibus if thirrsenuff fowk wantin tae gaun?"

"Actually, we've already been discussing the possibility of organising a trip through to the match", replied Jackie. "I'll put your name down".

Jackie's list for the trip through to the national stadium wasn't long in filling up; Tam Broon's mini-bus was duly booked, and the big day eventually arrived.

Sporting scarves, hats and rosettes in the black and gold colours of Wastby Wanderers, the excited supporters, including Rab Stewart and Jackie Campbell, waited at the agreed pick-up point for their transport to arrive.

However, there was one eager day-tripper who was not wearing the black and gold. In fact, he was wearing the red and white of CastleburghCity, Wastby's opponents on the day, and their long-standing bitter rivals. And that individual was Jimmy Walker.

"What's wi' the red an' white?" enquired Rab.

"It's 'cause ah'm a Castleburgh supporter, ayewees hiv been, eevir since ah played furrem!" replied Jimmy.

"You played for CastleburghCity? Away and Dinnae talk rubbish!" uttered Rab with a slightly raised voice.

This time, Jimmy's claim was so absurd that Rab simply hadn't been able to help himself from vociferously ridiculing the notion.

Castleburgh had for years and years been one of the top football teams in the country, and there was no way Rab was prepared to believe that Jimmy Walker had played for them. No, this time his far-fetched claim was bounding on the ridiculous.

"Ov coorse", continued Jimmy, "ah scored tha winnin' goal furrem whan they won rahcup in nineteen thurrtyfower".

Rab burst out laughing, and in doing so attracted the attention of all who were awaiting the arrival of the mini-bus.

"Are you seriously expecting us to believe", said Rab, as the other intending passengers listened with interest, "that you, Jimmy Walker, played football for Castleburgh?
And not only that. You also claim to have scored the winning goal when Castleburgh won the cup in nineteen-thirty-four?"

"Aye", replied Jimmy indignantly.

"An' ah wis their player o' rah year innaw!"

"You come out wi' some stories", said Rab; "but this one beats the lot!"

Tam Broon's mini-bus eventually arrived and the supporters hurriedly clambered aboard, most of them still shaking their heads at Jimmy's latest claim to fame, and all of them keen to secure a seat as far away from 'the haver' as possible.

Two hours later, the party arrived at their destination, parked up, and started to make their way towards the national stadium. As they got closer to the ground, the hordes of followers of both sides grew and grew, and eventually the streets around the ground became packed with thousands of football fans.

The atmosphere was now building up, and the Seadykes entourage eagerly soaked up the excitement as the kick-off time got closer and closer.

Then, just as they were passing the rear of the main grandstand, they observed a television crew arriving and being let in through a gate marked 'Players and Officials Only'.

"Here, is that not Joey Johnstone, the well-known football pundit and commentator?" remarked Jackie.

"I believe it is", replied Rab, who turned to the others and, raising his voice in order to be heard, said "hey, look over there, it's Joey Johnstone".

Rab hadn't meant to speak so loudly. To his embarrassment, the remark had actually been heard by the great man himself, who turned around and waved.

Then, to everyone's surprise, Joey Johnstone did a double take, and screwed up his eyes as he tried to focus in their direction.

"I don't believe it!" he proclaimed, before excusing himself from his colleagues and making his way across to where Jimmy Walker was standing.

"Well I never", exclaimed Joey Johnstone. "If it isn't Jimmy Walker".

Rab stared at Jackie with an expression of disbelief; and Jackie stared back with an equally intense look of incredulity.

"I haven't seen you for, let me see, maybe thirty years or more!" said the commentator.

"Aye, weel, its allangtyme sinssa geedup playin, Joey", replied Jimmy.

"Those were the days", reflected Joey. "I had only just started out on my career as a commentator back then. Of course all the commentaries were for the radio coverage back in those days".

Rab simply couldn't believe his ears.

"Excuse me, Mr. Johnstone", he butted in, "but are you saying you can actually remember Jimmy Walker playing football".

"Oh yes", replied Joey. "Jimmy here was one of the most exciting players I ever had the pleasure of commentating on back in the good old days before the war".

To say that Rab Stewart and Jackie Campbell had been rendered speechless was an understatement. You could have knocked them over with a feather.

"Well it's been nice speaking to you again Jimmy", said Joey. "Must dash though. Have to get myself set up for this afternoon's commentary".

"Aye, braw tae see ye as weel", replied Jimmy, as the pair shook hands.

Jackie nudged Rab.

"Well I never. All this time we've just let him haver on and never questioned the validity of his incredible stories. But the very time his seemingly unfeasible tale seems to be totally beyond belief, it turns out to be true!"

Rab looked at Jackie with a stunned expression. His mouth opened, but no words came out. He had, quite literally, been rendered speechless.

Joey Johnstone turned and headed back over towards the rear of the grandstand. But before disappearing through the 'Players and Officials Only' entrance, he turned towards Jimmy and shouted:

"And that winning goal you scored when CastleburghCity lifted the cup back in thirty-four. Has to be one of the best goals I ever saw!"

9

The Phantom Car

It was just before half-past-six on Saturday evening.

Jamie Strachan and best pal Mikey Mitchell were, as usual, waiting inside the shelter at the 'bus stop in Seadykes' Shore Street, from where they intended to board the six-thirty service to Kincraig, a village situated just over five miles up the coast.

This trip had become something of a habit in recent months. Ever since the two seventeen-year-olds had developed, despite being 'under-age', a liking for a pint on a Saturday night, they had been frequenting the Admiral's Arms in Kincraig. There they would down a few beers before returning on the last 'bus, which departed from the centre of the village at eleven.

To anyone not familiar with the peculiarities of the local area, travelling five miles up the coast on a Saturday night for a few pints might seem like a rather strange ritual. However, there was a very good reason for the pair having become regulars at the Admiral's Arms in Kincraig.

You see, the coastal town of Seadykes is a very close-knit community. Everybody knows everyone else's business; and, as a result, nobody can get away with even the slightest misdemeanor without every Tom, Dick and Harry getting to hear about it.

So, when it came to under-age-drinking, there was no chance of getting served in any of the Seadykes drinking establishments.

The bar staff at any pub in Seadykes would undoubtedly have known who you were, and that you hadn't yet reached that magical milestone that allowed you to drink alcohol legally.

And, even if the bar staff didn't know you, there would undoubtedly be someone in the pub who knew your parents and would spill the beans!

The village of Kincraig, however, was a different kettle of fish entirely. Hardly any of its residents had any connection with Seadykes or any of the other fishing villages dotted along the coast, as most of them had retired to the seaside village after having spent their entire careers in highly paid jobs in the city.

It was therefore more likely that an under-age drinker would be served in a Kincraig pub, especially if he looked a little older than his years and put on a deep voice in order to converse with the bar staff. Jamie Strachan fitted the bill perfectly, and so far no barman had ever refused to serve him!

This, of course, made him rather popular with his baby-faced peers, who relied on 'Big Jamie' to purchase their alcohol for them.

At precisely half-past-six, the 'bus drew in. Jamie and Mikey clambered aboard and made their way to their usual seat at the very back of the vehicle. Once the 'bus had moved off, the conductress made her way to the rear to collect their fares.

"A half tae Kincraig", said Mikey in a higher than usual pitch, as he slouched down in the seat trying to look as young as he possibly could.

"A half? What dae ye mean a half!" replied the conductress.

"You wis in my Johnny's class at the school, an' he's long past his seventeenth birthday! It's full fare for you now, m'lad, that'll be ninepence".

The problem that existed in the local pubs was also prevalent on the local public transport!

102

The conductress turned the handle on her machine and out popped the ninepenny ticket. Mikey reluctantly handed over the money.

"And the same for you?" enquired the conductress as she stared at Jamie. There was no way he could possibly chance a reduced fare after Mikey had been refused, and Jamie was also forced to part with his ninepence.

A short while later the 'bus drew up at the stance in the centre of Toreness, the neighbouring village, where two pals of Jamie and Mikey, Pete Paterson and Alfie Anderson, boarded the vehicle.

"How's it gaun, lads?" shouted Jamie from the back seat.

"All right, Jas!" came the reply, as Pete and Alfie made their way to the rear to join their chums.

"I wouldny bother tryin' for a half ticket", advised Mikey. "The conductress knows who we are and she knows we're too old for a half-fare".

"Ach, that means less beer money then", bemoaned Alfie.

Ten minutes later, the 'bus arrived in Kincraig, and the four pals disembarked before making their way down to the pub.

Situated on the front street overlooking the harbour, the Admiral's Arms was an old fashioned establishment, with a low entrance door and low ceilings. The interior reeked excitingly of spilled beer and stale tobacco smoke, and the décor was well stained with nicotine, having not seen the decorator's paint brush for many a year.

Once inside, Mikey, Pete and Alfie scurried through to a table at the back of the poorly-lit tavern, where their youthful looks would hopefully be less conspicuous. Jamie, however, made his way to the bar and, being the more mature looking of the four, had no trouble in ordering up four pints of heavy.

As the barman poured the pints, Jamie chuckled to himself as he recalled Mikey's first failed attempt to get served, when he had asked for "two pints of alcohol". Needless to say, the naïve youth had been quickly ejected from the premises with the threat of a size-ten boot up his backside!

There had been no such problem getting served tonight, however. Skilfully holding the four pints between his two hands, Jamie made his way back through to the rear of the pub where his pals were seated,

"My that tastes good!" exclaimed Mikey, after having taken a long thirst-quenching slug from his glass.

"Sure does", replied Pete, before reaching inside his denim jacket to pull out a packet of cigarettes, which were then passed around. If the truth be told, Jamie and Mikey weren't smokers, but they accepted the offer anyway in the mistaken belief that it made them look that little bit older!

Before long, the four pint glasses stood empty on the table, and Jamie collected money from the other three before making his way back over to the bar for the second round.

Standing at the bar, as the barman filled the glasses, he heard the front door open and turned around nervously to see who had just entered the pub. There was always the chance on a Saturday night that the local police would be on their occasional under-age drinking patrol!

To his relief, it wasn't the police who had walked in, but two females, one of whom, Mandy Murray, Jamie had admired for a very long time, despite the fact that she was almost a year his senior.

Mandy had been in the year ahead of Jamie at school, and she was a Kincraig girl; the village being situated in the SeadykesAcademy geographical catchment area.

Being a late child, Mandy had enjoyed a rather spoiled upbringing. She lived with her elderly parents, who had retired to Kincraig about five years ago, in a house on the other side of the village from the Admiral's Arms.

As well as being 'a bit of a looker', it was well known that Mandy's family weren't short of a bob or two; which, it has to be said, made her even more of a 'catch', as she always seemed to have more money to splash around than most girls of her age.

"Hiya Mandy", Jamie shouted, at the same time aware that his cheeks had started to flush.

"Hey, look, it's Jamie", Mandy whispered to her companion, Senga Stewart. "Will we say hello?"

"Aye, why not" replied Senga, and the two girls joined Jamie at the bar.

"Are you here on your own?" enquired Mandy.

"No, I'm with Mikey, Pete and Alfie. They're sitting right at the back there, trying to blend in with the surroundings. You can join us if you like".

"Don't mind if we do" said Mandy. "We'll get a couple of ciders and be right over".

Before long, after the beer and cider had loosened their tongues, the jokes and amusing anecdotes were pouring out. And, as the alcohol started to take a firm hold, Jamie's confidence grew as his inhibitions all but disappeared.

Slowly, he edged along the bench seat, and moved up closer and closer to Mandy. He had longed for an opportunity such as this, and to his pleasant surprise Mandy was showing little sign of resistance.

In fact, she seemed to be enjoying his mild advances!

As the beer and cider flowed, the humour became more bawdy and ribald, but the girls didn't seem to mind. They were both laughing just as loud as the lads, and seemed to be really enjoying their night.

Then, Alfie Anderson suddenly changed the subject. He was the sort of guy who enjoyed a bit of a wind up, and never missed the opportunity to relate a tall-tale, especially when in the company of semi-inebriated companions.

Above all, he enjoyed scaring the girls with spooky yarns.

"By the way, did any of you hear about the phantom car?" he probed.

"Away, there's no such thing", retorted Senga.

"Well, seemingly", Alfie continued, "there's a ghostly car that's been seen on several occasions recently between Kincraig and St. Dronans. Usually about half-eleven at night".

Pete, realising that Alfie was on the wind-up, was all too ready to back up his pal.

"I heard about that as well", he cut in. "Apparently, there was a car went missing around these parts a few years ago, and it was last seen on that very stretch of road. The car and its two occupants were never traced, and they reckon the driver must have lost control and went over the cliff".

"But surely the wreck of the car would eventually have been found at the bottom of the cliff?" Mandy pointed out.

"No chance", replied Alfie. "There's always huge waves crashing in on that part of the coast, which create strong under-currents that head back offshore. These currents would, in all probability, have dragged what remained of the car and its occupants far out into deep water".

From the horrified looks on the faces of those seated around the table, Alfie knew that his latest leg-pulling exercise was working a treat. His audience looked like they were being taken in hook, line and sinker!

The tale was spooking Mandy to the extent that she started to edge closer to Jamie, much to his delight. To reassure her, Jamie put his arm around Mandy's waist, and was pleasantly surprised to find she offered little resistance.

If the truth be told, Jamie also found such tales unsettling, and found comfort in Mandy's close proximity!

"So, how does this apparition manifest itself?" enquired Mikey, with a slight hint of skepticism.

"It's the headlights they always see first", explained Alfie, elaborating on the fantasy as he spoke. "Seemingly, the eyewitnesses see the headlights first, then hear a screech of tyres, then a scream, then a splash".

"Come off it, you're winding us up!" exclaimed Jamie. "I've never heard so much rubbish in my life!"

"Well, if you choose not to believe it, that's entirely up to you", advised Alfie. "I'm only telling you what I heard from a very reliable source, er . . who wants to remain anonymous for fear of ridicule".

"Anyway, enough of that nonsense", Mikey cut in, looking at his watch. "Time for one more round before we go for the 'bus? Get them in Jamie!"

Jamie stood up to make his way to the bar. "Hold on, I'll give you a hand", said Mandy, who rose from her seat and brushed past the others. After managing to push their way through the drinkers who were milling around the bar, Jamie caught the attention of the barman and ordered up the final round of the evening.

As they waited on the drinks to arrive, Jamie turned to Mandy. His confidence boosted with half-a-gallon of ale, he asked if he could walk her home. There should be just enough time to get to Mandy's house and back to the 'bus stop before the last service departed at eleven.

"I just thought you'd be a wee bit frightened walking through the dark streets after listening to Alfie's scary ghost story", he explained, tongue firmly in cheek.

"You can walk me home, but that's all!" replied Mandy, as she wagged a finger at him in a jocular fashion. "And you'll have to hurry back to the 'bus stop after seeing me home if you don't want to have to walk all the way back to Seadykes".

After carrying the drinks back over to where the others were seated, Jamie and Mandy downed theirs as quickly as they could before making their excuses and starting to head towards the door.

"Remember, the last 'bus is at eleven", Mikey advised Jamie as he brushed past. "And it's just after ten now!"

"Dinnae worry, I'll no' be long. Ah'm just walking Mandy to her door, then I'll hurry right back tae the 'bus stop."

The cold air hit Mandy and Jamie as soon as they stepped out on to the street, with a fresh breeze blowing in off the sea and across the harbour. In the distance, they could hear the waves crashing off the back of the sea wall.

"Looks like a storm is getting up" remarked Mandy, "and the wind's biting through this thin raincoat".

Jamie put his arm around her as they made their way towards Mandy's house, which was around a fifteen minute walk away, in the opposite direction from the 'bus stop. Mandy cuddled into him.

Walking as fast as they could, they eventually arrived at Mandy's house; which, to her apparent surprise, was in darkness.

"There's no lights on. Looks like my mum and dad have gone out", she observed. "Come to think of it, I did hear my dad mention something about a function down at the golf club. I bet that's where they've gone. And once my dad starts reminiscing with the other members about memorable rounds of golf they've had over the years, there's no stopping him".

Mandy turned to face Jamie.

"They won't be home any time soon. Look, it's about a twenty minute walk from here back to the 'bus stop. I don't suppose there's any harm in me inviting you in for a quick coffee? Just a coffee, though," she said with a cheeky smile as she waved her finger in his face, just like she had done in the pub.

"It'll have to be a very quick one then", said Jamie. "Last thing I want on a night like this is to have to walk all the way home!"

Mandy let them in, hung up her coat, and proceeded towards the kitchenette, where she filled a kettle and put it on the gas stove. Jamie, meanwhile, sat himself down on the settee.

A couple of minutes later, Mandy walked back through carrying two cups of sweet milky coffee, handed one to Jamie, and sat herself down next to him on the settee.

With both of them still feeling the effects of the alcohol, conversation came easily; and, as they chatted away, they lost all track of time.

Suddenly, about a quarter-of-an-hour later, Jamie remembered that he had a twenty-minute walk back to the 'bus stop and glanced at his watch.

To his horror, it was nearly ten-to-eleven!

"Oh, no!" shouted Jamie. "Sorry, Mandy, ah've got tae go, I'll have tae run!"

He stood up, pulled on his coat, gave Mandy a peck on the cheek, and made for the door.

"If you run fast enough you might just catch it", she shouted after him as he disappeared down the garden path.

Jamie ran through the dark, cold streets as fast as he could, but the alcohol was making him unsteady on his feet, and on several occasions he had to pull up and rest against a wall.

Eventually, he reached the centre of the village, but just as the 'bus stop came into view, he saw the last service of the evening drawing away. He ran after it, shouting, but to no avail. He had missed the last 'bus home, and now he was going to have to walk.

Resigning himself to the arduous hike that lay ahead, Jamie rested for a few minutes in the relative comfort of the 'bus stance shelter to regain his breath, before setting out on the five-mile trek back to Seadykes.

It had started to rain now and, with the wind strengthening, it looked like he was in for a miserable footslog. Unless, of course, he could hitch a lift!

Venturing out into the darkness, he pulled up his hood and kept his head down. Very soon, the village lights faded behind him, and Jamie listened out for the sound of cars approaching from the rear, ready to stick out his thumb if the opportunity arose.

Thick woods on either side of the road at this point made it almost pitch black, and it was difficult to see the footpath as it stretched into the distance. The wind was really getting up now, and the noise of the tree branches being blown around was quite frightening.

On and on he walked, but the sound of an approaching vehicle never came.

Thankfully, when he was about half-a-mile from the village, Jamie found himself clear of the woods, where it didn't seem quite so creepy; and, when the moon occasionally broke through the clouds, he was just about able to make out where he was putting his feet.

Then, suddenly, the road ahead of him seemed to be lit up by the headlights of a car approaching from the rear.

His spirits raised, Jamie kept walking with his thumb stuck out as he waited for the car, or lorry, or whatever it was, to pull up beside him. But what he hoped would be a welcome lift home never materialised.

He turned around and looked back towards Kincraig, only to find himself staring into inky blackness. There was nothing there. The car headlights must have been a figment of his imagination!

Dejected, Jamie pulled up his collar once again and resumed his long march home, with the driving rain blowing into his face. By now he was well and truly miserable.

It was becoming painfully difficult to keep his arm extended in order to thumb a lift. But as the howling wind would surely have drowned out the sound of an approaching car, he had no other option. He couldn't just wait until he thought he heard the sound of an engine before sticking out his arm. He had to keep thumbing away, painful as it was.

If only he hadn't accepted Mandy's offer of a coffee. If only he'd set out in plenty of time for the 'bus stop. Jamie had longed for the time that he could be alone with Mandy, even just for a moment; but now he was paying a heavy price for that all too brief flirtation!

Then, just like before, the road ahead of him was lit up by a beam from behind. Surely he'd be picked up by a sympathetic motorist this time!

Again, however, no vehicle of any description pulled up beside him or passed him by. And, once again, Jamie turned around and peered back in the direction of the village, but there was nothing there. He was now starting to doubt his own sanity.

Turning around to face the wind and rain, he trudged on; and, to keep his spirits up he thought back to earlier in the evening, when Mandy had allowed him to put his arm around her. He smiled within himself as he remembered how she'd cuddled into him in the pub, when Alfie was telling that stupid story about the phantom car.

A phantom car! How ridiculous was that? There was obviously no substance to such far-fetched tales. After all, there was no such thing as ghosts!

Once again the road ahead was lit up by the lights of a vehicle approaching from behind, and once again Jamie waited in expectation before eventually turning around to find that no car was approaching.

His imagination then started to run riot.

Could there actually be such a thing as a phantom car? Was the story more than just hearsay? Was it the headlights of Alfie's ghostly car that had been lighting up the road in front of him? He thought back to what Alfie had said.

A ghostly car, usually seen about half-past eleven between Kincraig and St. Dronans. The first thing that the eyewitnesses recalled seeing seen was the headlights! No, surely there was no substance to such stories. He tried to block it from his mind.

But suddenly, the road ahead of Jamie was lit up once again, just like before, with what he could swear was car headlights approaching from the rear. Turning around once again, this time with the seeds sown in his mind that there just might be some truth in far-fetched tale of the ghostly car, he found himself staring once again into nothing but inky blackness.

He was very tired now. He was cold and wet, and growing more and more fearful of the dark. And he was getting frightened. Fighting back the tears, Jamie sat down on the low stone wall that skirted the footpath. Surely it was just the darkness that was playing tricks with his mind? Nevertheless, he was becoming increasingly terrified!

Maybe he should start heading back towards Kincraig? Maybe Mandy would take pity on him and, with her parents' permission, let him stay for the night?

Yes, that was the answer. That was the best course of action. Surely her parents wouldn't turn him away on a night like this. They lived in a big posh house, with plenty of big posh rooms. Surely it wouldn't impose on them too much to offer him a bed. He would be up and away home on the first 'bus the following morning.

Jamie stood up and started to head back towards the village. Then, all of a sudden, he was almost blinded by a fierce beam of light; so fierce that he was forced to close his eyes.

Only after the light had faded away did he feel it was safe to open them again. But all that he could see was the same inky blackness.

Jamie decided that he had had enough of this nonsense. It was time to come to his senses. There was no such thing as ghosts, there was no such thing as the phantom car, and he was going to prove it.

Patiently, he waited for the light to come again, ready this time to shield his eyes from the dazzling beam and ascertain its source.

Then, exactly thirty seconds after the last dazzling shaft of light, the blinding flash manifested itself again. But this time, with his eyes narrowed to slits and with his hand deflecting the worst of the glare, the mystery was solved.

And, despite being cold, wet and miserable, Jamie almost burst out laughing. What he had initially been sure was an approaching vehicle, but had then feared was the fabled ghostly car, was simply nothing more sinister than the beam from the Kincraig Ness lighthouse, which swept over the surrounding landscape regular as clockwork, twice every minute!

10

Cutting Off His Nose to Spite His Face

"Almost home now!" Robbie Falconer shouted over to crew mate and best pal Willie Wilson, as the 'Pole Star', a fifty-five foot seine netter, finally reached the calmer waters of the estuary.

The two young deck hands had just spent a grueling three days and nights at sea in search of haddock, and were looking forward to a spell, albeit a brief one, on dry land.

It had been a hard trip, and the fishing had been mediocre, but very soon the boat would be back in Seadykes harbour; the catch would be unloaded onto the back of a waiting lorry before being taken to market; and both Robbie and Willie could finally make their way home to the comfort of their warm beds.

For the moment, however, the two pals, along with fellow crew member Lachlan Watt, a seaman of many years experience, were tasked with gutting the fish on a cold and exposed deck before packing them in wooden boxes, ready to be unloaded once the boat had reached the harbour.

Both Robbie and Willie were still rather young and naïve; or, to coin a phrase, 'a little wet behind the ears'. During their schooldays, a part of their lives that, in their opinion, had ended none too soon at the age of fifteen, neither had taken their education seriously.

Like most other local laddies of their age, it was their belief that a lifelong career as a fisherman awaited them, and when had a deck hand ever needed qualifications?

That was just three years ago; and, in those three years, both had learned the hard way that the life of a fisherman is tough and brutal, and not one that should be desired.

"Robbie!" shouted skipper and boat owner Calum Cameron through the open window of the wheelhouse, to where Robbie was leaning against the winch.

"Move yersel', there plenty o' fish tae clean yet, and you know as weel as I do they're worth more gutted than whole".

"Aye, gaffer. I wis just haein' a breather".

"Well get a move on," came the reply. "We'll be hame in half an hour, an' the fish lorry will be waitin' on the pier!"

Reluctantly, the chastised deck hand returned to his task of gutting the fish.

"Aye, and what dae you know", he muttered under his breath. "Ah'll get the boxes packed in my ain good time. Just you steer the boat, and I'll dae a' the hard work".

If there was one thing that Robbie hated, it was being ordered around. All of his working life he had resented being at the beck and call of his so-called superiors.

Oh, how he wished he had a better job. A job where he wouldn't have to endure gale force winds; a job where he wouldn't have to look out for waves crashing along the deck that could easily carry him over the side to a watery grave; and one where he wouldn't have to suffer the bitter cold that made his fingers so numb that he couldn't even feel the blade of the gutting knife as it made yet another incision on the end of his thumb.

If only he had paid attention at school. If only he hadn't let his stubbornness rule his life at an early age, when he rarely paid attention to lessons and habitually failed to return his homework.

And it was all because he hated being told what to do. But surely, if he didn't want to listen and he didn't want to learn, that was up to him, wasn't it? Surely he was entitled to live his life as he chose, not as others dictated!

Eventually, the Pole Star arrived in Seadykes harbour, where Robbie, Willie and Lachlan helped secure the vessel to the pier. They then started to unload the catch, with Lachlan in charge of the winch; Robbie tasked with hooking the boxes of fish on to the derrick rope; and Willie designated the duty of standing on the back of the lorry to catch the boxes as they were swung over.

"I hope the market prices are better than they were last week, Lachie," remarked Robbie as he attached three boxes of haddock, piled one on top of the another, to the grabs on the end of the derrick rope.

"Aye, ah hope so", replied Lachlan. "It was a poor catch and a poor pay last week. Mind you, by the looks of it, this'll not be much better".

Lachlan wrapped the end of the derrick rope around the winch and allowed the mechanism to take the strain and raise the three boxes of fish high in the air before they were swung over on to the back of the lorry. Unfortunately, Willie failed to grab the load properly after it had traversed the gap between the boat and the pier, causing a few haddock to spill out and fall into the harbour.

Skipper Calum Cameron stuck his head out of the wheelhouse window, and bellowed at the unfortunate Willie.

"If you would pay mair care an' attention tae yer job, Willie, we wouldna' be losin' oor hard-won catch over the side! Noo, buck up yer ideas, an' get a move on!"

"Sorry skipper, it'll no' happen again" shouted Willie from the back of the lorry.

"Why don't ye just tug yer forelock and be done wi' it", muttered Robbie, once the skipper was out of earshot. "Ye would think he was Lord o' the Manor, the way he speaks doon tae us from his high and mighty perch in that wheelhoose".

"Well, that's as may be", Lachlan interrupted. "But ye've tae mind he's the man that pays oor wages". Years of experience had taught old Lachlan Watt that you should never bite the hand that feeds!

Finally, the catch was unloaded, and the lorry made off for the fish market. The crew of the Pole Star, all except for Calum Cameron, started to make their way home. The skipper's day would not be finished until he had seen the fish sold at the market, and the proceeds of the trip safely in his pocket. It was only then, after he knew how much the fish had sold for, and had deducted the boat's expenses, that he could work out how much his crew could be paid for the trip.

Both Robbie and Willie were tired and weary after having spent three nights away from home. During this time they had grabbed what little sleep they could in the cramped box beds located within the confined living quarters below deck in the stern of the vessel. With the boat constantly rising and falling in the heavy sea, and with incessant diesel fumes emanating from the adjacent engine room, conditions had been far from pleasant and sleep near impossible.

However, they could both put all that to the back of their minds for now. It was Friday afternoon; they wouldn't have to go back to sea until Monday, and they had the whole weekend to enjoy. And with both Robbie and Willie being keen footballers with the local side, Seadykes Athletic, they had a home 'derby' match against local rivals Toreness Rovers to look forward to on Saturday afternoon.

For now, though, all they could think about was to get home to a hot dinner, a bath, and a couple of hours kip. Then, being

Friday, the pair would no doubt head off down to their local, the Sailor's Return, for a few pints. With any luck there might be a live band playing in the hall through the back, and there might be hordes of gorgeous females in attendance just waiting to be 'pulled'.

And that was how their night panned out. It turned out there was a band playing, and more than a few pints were consumed. As for the fairer sex, however, their attempts at wooing the women, as usual, failed miserably!

The following day, after both had enjoyed a lie in to sleep off the previous night's beer, Willie called for Robbie and the pair made their way along to SkellyPark, the home ground of Seadykes Athletic.

The local Football and Athletic Club had been founded some eighty years earlier, in order 'to promote the health and well being of local sports enthusiasts'. And, in those early days, Seadykes Athletic had enjoyed success as one of the most prominent clubs in the district.

A gift of land from Lord Skelly, the local laird, along with a substantial donation to club funds, had allowed Seadykes Athletic to set up home at the appropriately named SkellyPark, which they proceeded to enclose with a wooden fence. Eventually, a small terrace was built up to accommodate the increasing number of spectators who were warming to the game of Association football in the late nineteenth century.

The club's efforts were rewarded when, in 1889, they reached the fourth round of the Scottish Cup; a remarkable achievement for a village side! Some of the older Seadykes supporters, who were only young laddies at the time, still had fond memories at that cup run.

They were of the staunch opinion that the Athletic had been unfortunate to have exited the competition by the narrowest of margins to one of the 'big guns' from the west.

The gate money from the crowds that had packed into SkellyPark during the cup run enabled the club to fund the construction of a small wooden grandstand, which was opened amidst much celebration at the start of the following season.

In recent years, however, with crowds dwindling, the football ground had been allowed to fall into disrepair. Several gaps had started to appear in the perimeter fence, allowing free entry to young boys or anyone else slim enough to slip through if no club official was around. The once neat terracing was now covered in grass and weeds, and the old grandstand afforded little shelter on a rainy day.

Dark clouds may have descended on SkellyPark in recent times, but the club had seen much brighter performances on the field of play since Robbie and Willie had broken into the side. Known locally as 'The Dynamic Duo', a moniker no doubt stolen from the 'Batman and Robin' television series, centre-forward Willie Wilson and inside-right Robbie Falconer had netted no fewer than thirty-six goals so far this season, largely due to the pair having operated a slick 'one-two' tactic that never failed to catch out their opponents' defence.

Arriving at SkellyPark forty-five minutes before the scheduled kick-off time, Robbie and Willie made their way to the pavilion, where the usual banter was exchanged with the players who had already arrived and were in the process of changing into their football strips.

Ten minutes later, the pair were out on the park going through their usual pre-match shooting practice routine.

"How many today, lads?" shouted Davie Wilson from his usual vantage point behind the goals.

"Five for me and five for Robbie during the first half", answered Willie. "Then we'll just take oor foot aff the pedal for the second forty-five so that we dinnae embarrass the Toreness's too much".

"Oh aye, right you are then", replied Davie, believing every word.

However, Toreness Rovers had also had a good season so far, and the local rivals were sitting second in the league table, just a point behind the Athletic. The match was never going to be as one-sided as Willie's tongue-in-cheek prediction had suggested! It turned out to be a comfortable victory nonetheless, with Willie scoring twice and Robbie once in a three-nil win.

Unbeknown to Robbie and Willie, there had been one unfamiliar face amongst the sparse gathering of spectators at Skelly Park that afternoon; a spectator who had been more than keen to see the Dynamic Duo in action. That spectator was a talent scout from Wastby Wanderers, the senior club based about ten miles up the coast.

After Robbie and Willie had showered and dressed, amidst the shenanigans and skylarking that were always in abundance following a victory, the Athletic coach called them into his office.

There, seated behind the desk, was the stranger who had looked on as the pair had, yet again, executed their 'one-two' goal scoring routine with such precision. The stranger had been more than impressed with their performance.

"Please take a seat, gentlemen, and allow me to introduce myself".

Robbie and Willie exchanged glances, before sitting down on the two chairs that had been placed on the opposite side of the desk from the stranger.

"My name is Jocky Thomson, and I'm a talent scout for Wastby Wanderers. We were tipped off about the goal scoring prowess of you two young lads, and I was sent along to take a look.

I have to tell you now that I was very impressed with what I saw, and I have the Wanderers' authority to invite you both along to Wastby for a trial. If you are in agreement, the club would like to try you out in a reserve match this coming Monday evening. What do you say?"

There was a brief pause as Robbie and Willie allowed what the stranger had just said to sink in.

"We're both fishermen, and we're due to go back to sea on Monday morning", replied Willie. "If we miss the trip we'll probably lose our jobs".

Robbie, however, viewed the situation very differently.

"Mr. Thomson, if the trial is successful, and Wastby decide to take us on, how much will we be paid?"

"That all depends on the contract", replied the scout.

"What I can tell you, however, is that it will be a part-time agreement. Having said that, the club has 'connections' with a number of local businesses; in fact, several of these business owners are directors of Wastby Wanderers, and it would be no trouble to find you both part-time positions to supplement your footballers' wages.

In addition, the club owns several properties where out-of-town players are accommodated. You would both be given a room, which would, of course, be rent-free".

This was music to Robbie's ears. If he signed for Wastby Wanderers, there would be no more sleep-deprived nights on the open sea, and no more bitterly cold days spent hauling nets and gutting fish.

"That sounds good enough for me", said Robbie, before he turned to look at Willie. "What about you".

Willie, although just a shade dubious and afraid that things might not work out, decided that if Robbie was prepared to take the risk, then so was he!

"Aye, count me in too. What time do you want us along on Monday?"

"It's a seven-thirty kick off, so we'll see you at six o'clock prompt!"

Monday couldn't come quickly enough. After having advised a rather irate Calum Cameron that they wouldn't be going to sea on the Pole Star that day, or possibly any other day for that matter, Robbie and Willie made their way up to the railway station, where they boarded the 16:25 for Wastby Central. Settling into their seats as the train steamed up the incline out of Seadykes, Willie turned to face Robbie.

"Do you think this could be the turning point in our lives, Rob? Do you think we'll be able to say cheerio and good riddance to the fishing?"

"Well I for one am determined that I will never again have to make my way down to the harbour with my kit bag slung over my shoulder. Once I start banging in the goals for Wastby, I'm sure some big club from down south will come in for me, and I'll secure my future in the game".

"That's a nice thought", replied Willie. "But we can't get too carried away. If Wastby do decide to sign us, then we'll just have to see how it pans out from there. If they don't, then I'm not so sure we'll get our berths back on the Pole Star!"

"Why let that worry you", said Robbie. "There are plenty of other fishing boats working out of Seadykes. We wouldn't be out of work for long".

Eventually, the train arrived at its destination, where the Dynamic Duo alighted before making their way on foot to PitheadPark, the home ground of Wastby Wanderers, where they arrived just after half-past-five.

PitheadPark was what you could call a traditional Scottish provincial football ground. Built up in dribs and drabs over the years since the club had been founded just after the turn of the century, it consisted of three sides of terracing, built up with ash and rubble and lined with old railway sleepers. Along the other side was situated an old corrugated-iron clad grandstand.

Robbie and Willie, who were at this stage starting to feel just a little nervous, entered the ground through an open door in the rear of the grandstand, where they immediately bumped into Jocky Thomson.

"That's what I like to see, nice and punctual", remarked Jocky. "We can't abide bad timekeeping here at Wastby Wanderers, and we like our players to be disciplined. You two have made a good start! Come on, I'll introduce you to the gaffer".

Jocky led the way along a narrow corridor, where he hesitated momentarily in front of a door on which was emblazoned in bold capitals: 'MANAGER'; beneath which callers were advised in no uncertain terms to 'Knock and WAIT'.

Jocky knocked gently on the door, and awaited a response. After a brief pause, a firm voice from within told them to enter. Jocky opened the door and put his head around it, before announcing "the two lads from Seadykes are here, Mr. McPherson".

The trio silently made their way into the office, where they were met with the distinct odour of pipe tobacco.

Sitting behind a rather old antique-looking desk in an old leather-bound chair was the formidable figure of Alex McPherson, the Wastby manager. He removed his pipe from his mouth and looked up.

"So this is the Seadykes 'goal-scoring machine' that everyone up the coast is raving about! Well, lads, on the recommendation of Mr. Thomson here we're prepared to give you a trial. If you impress us enough, we'll consider offering you a contract. If we do see fit to sign you on, and you keep your noses clean, so to speak, there could well be a future in the game for you. That's all for now, away and get changed. You'll wear the number eight and number nine jerseys, just like you do for the Seadykes club. I'll see you both again for the team talk fifteen minutes before kick-off".

Robbie and Willie made their way to the dressing room as instructed, and started to change into the football kit that had been neatly hung on pegs that corresponded with the shirt numbers.

"Here's our strips" announced Willie, before seating himself beneath the number nine peg. Robbie sat beside him.

"Who does that geyser think he is?" muttered Robbie. "I won't be spoken to in that sort of tone. The man who gets me to toe the line has yet to be born!"

"Come on, Robbie. He's the manager. The gaffer. You have to do as he says if you want to play for the Wanderers".

"Aye, well, we'll see about that" replied Robbie, more in bravado than anything else. He knew as well as Willie that he would have to conform. At least to begin with!

The rest of the team, which consisted mainly of a mixture of seasoned regulars coming back from injury and youngsters who were still trying to break into the first team squad, entered the changing room in dribs and drabs and introduced themselves.

The reserve team captain, Sammy Simpson, shook their hands.

"Have you played under floodlights before?" enquired Sammy.

"You're kidding", replied Willie. "We've only ever played amateur football before!"

Sammy smiled. "I think you'll find this a wee bit different. The game will be faster, and you won't get much time on the ball. And about the lights, you'll find it difficult to see high balls when you're looking up into them. You'll have to learn to anticipate where the ball is going to drop. That's all I can think to tell you for now, but the main thing is to remember that I'm the team captain. If you keep listening to my advice, then you'll be okay".

Sammy turned to the other players.

"Right lads, let's get out there and get warmed up".

As they made their way down the tunnel, Robbie turned to Willie.

"Another one that likes the sound o' his ain voice!"

"Acht, Robbie! Haud yer wheesht. Sammy Simpson has years o' experience in the senior game. Let's just tak' his advice and be done wi' it!"

Twenty-five minutes later, with their warm up complete, the players returned to the dressing room, where manager McPherson stood in front of a tactics board awaiting their return.

"Right lads, sit yersel down. Here's how we're going to approach tonight's game. First of all, we have two proven goal-scorers on trial from Seadykes Athletic. I'm advised they play well off each other, and tonight they'll be spearheading the attack".

Robbie and Willie exchanged glances. They both knew that this was going to be their big chance. The manager continued with his team talk.

"We know that our opponents tonight, Strathforth, are going to be weak down the right flank. At every opportunity, exploit this weakness. Outside right - do your very best get the ball down the wing before squaring it to centre, where hopefully our two trialists can finish the job".

The players listened intently to the remainder of the talk, after which captain Sammy Simpson stood up and shouted "right lads, you've heard what the manager has to say, now let's get out there and do the business!"

Robbie and Willie's trial went like a dream. Time and again, the weaknesses in the Strathforth side were exploited, and the Dynamic Duo were allowed to play their renowned 'one-two' goal-scoring tactic to great effect.

When the final whistle sounded, Wastby reserves had beaten their Strathforth counterparts by three goals without reply, with Robbie having netted twice and Willie once.

Indeed, had it not been for some fantastic saves from the Strathie 'keeper, the winning margin could have been far greater.

Manager Alex McPherson couldn't get the lads to put pen to paper quickly enough. As the ink dried on their signatures, he reclined in his big leather chair and allowed a rare smile to spread across his face, before looking up.

"Welcome to Wastby Wanderers, boys. I think this will be the beginning of very successful professional football careers for you both".

As the weeks progressed, it looked very much like the manager's prediction was correct.

It didn't take long for Robbie and Willie to establish themselves in the first team, and before long their goal-scoring prowess made them terracing favourites, even amongst the most diehard and critical followers of the club. Behind the scenes, however, Robbie was beginning to ruffle a few feathers.

As usual, his stubbornness and refusal to follow the rules was starting to rub certain club officials up the wrong way. It was Wastby Wanderers' club policy that every player, whether arriving at PitheadPark on a Saturday for a home match or travelling on the team 'bus, would wear the club blazer and tie. This was just the sort of rule that Robbie Falconer loved to flaunt.

"Where's your tie?" bellowed manager McPherson one Saturday as he met Robbie at the dressing room door.

"Must have mislaid it", replied Robbie in an all-too nonchalant manner.

Robbie brushed past the gaffer, and started to slip out of his blazer as he approached the peg where his number eight shirt was hanging.

Suddenly, he felt a presence directly behind him.

"FALCONER! AM I HURTING YOU?"

Robbie nearly jumped out of his skin; and, with a puzzled expression, turned to face the manager.

"No, you're not hurting me", he replied.

"WELL I SHOULD BE, BECAUSE I AM STANDING ON YOUR HAIR. YOU LOOK LIKE A BEATNIK. GET IT CUT BEFORE YOU COME TO TRAINING ON WEDNESDAY NIGHT. DO I MAKE MYSELF CLEAR?"

Robbie gave a half-hearted nod, before turning back to face the wall.

There was no way he was going to be dictated to, especially when it came to how long he chose to wear his hair. Was long hair not the latest fashion? It wasn't his fault if Alex McPherson wasn't prepared to move with the times.

Of course, when he turned up for the midweek training session, Robbie's hair was still far too long for the gaffer's liking.

"Where's your guitar, son?" enquired the manager when Robbie walked into the dressing room.

"My guitar?" replied Robbie. "I don't know what you mean".

"Oh, it's you, Falconer. For a minute I thought you were one of the Beatles. NOW TAKE THIS AS A FINAL WARNING. GET YOUR HAIR CUT BEFORE SATURDAY. I CAN'T HAVE MY TEAM RUNNING OUT ON TO THE PARK LOOKING LIKE A LOT OF LONG-HAIRED NELLIES!"

And so it went on. Robbie continued to get on the wrong side of everyone at the club, and not just the manager. On the field of play, although he continued to bang in the goals, he constantly turned a deaf ear to the team captain's instructions.

As for the rest of his team mates, they knew only too well that it was pointless trying to put over their point of view. It was Robbie's way, or nothing.

Eventually, towards the end of the season, things came to a head. The Wanderers were, largely thanks to Robbie and Willie's goal-scoring expertise, challenging for the league championship.

With just three games to go, they were sitting at the top of the table, one point ahead of nearest challengers Ferryport, who also happened to be their next opponents.

On the day of the crucial match that would, in all probability, decide the championship, manager Alex McPherson set out his stall after the players had completed their warm up.

"Right, lads, here's how we're going to play it. If we can hold Ferryport to a draw, then we'll still be leading the pack with two matches to play, which I'm sure I don't have to remind you are against teams from the lower half of the league.

In other words, if we don't lose to Ferryport, we'll be red-hot favourites for the league flag. In order to giver us the best possible chance of avoiding defeat, I'm going to re-shuffle the side a bit."

The players exchanged glances. They were mostly well disciplined and ready to accept change, but at the same time they were fearful for what Robbie Falconer's reaction might be if the proposed changes involved him. They listened intently as the manager continued.

"I'm going to play a defensive formation. Falconer, you have a big physical presence – I want you to sit back in midfield, and occasionally drop into defence if the need arises. That way, we'll make it very difficult for the opposition to score.

Wilson – I know this may sound like a tall order, but I'd like you to play up front on your own, where hopefully you can make the most of any long ball that might come your way. And remember, lads, defence is the name of the game this afternoon. Don't let me down!"

Robbie couldn't believe his ears. McPherson was splitting up their striking partnership. He obviously didn't have a clue what he was doing!

PitheadPark was full to overflowing when the players ran down the tunnel and on to the pitch. The supporters had turned out in their droves for the match, in the full knowledge that a good result would go a long way to securing Wastby's first league title for over twenty years.

The atmosphere was electric!

The game started with both sides looking nervous; but, as time progressed, the home team started to look more comfortable on the ball. The manager's tactics of closing down the opposition looked to be working; and Robbie, for once, appeared to be doing as he was told.

Half-time arrived with neither team having found the net.

"We're half-way there; we just need to keep playing as we are, and the job's done", manager McPherson advised the players during the half-time team talk. "I'm pleased to see you're all following my instructions. Let's keep it that way".

The team started the second half just as they had finished the first forty-five, and all seemed to be going well. However, as the minutes ticked by, Robbie started to get restless in his defensive role. In his opinion, the game was there to be won.

Surely there would be no harm in one venture up-field, where a quick 'one-two' with Willie would catch the opposition unawares and net the goal that would surely win full points for the Wanderers? Aye, he would show McPherson how the game should be played!

Robbie seized his moment when possession had been won wide on the right. Shouting for the pass as he moved forward, the ball was played to his feet and he sprinted up the park, with Willie to his left. Then, just as Robbie was about to play his trade-mark one-two manoeuvre with his established striking partner, the ball hit a divot and he lost possession.

Ferryport immediately turned defence into attack, and exposed the weakness left by Robbie's foray up-field. The ball found its way through to their centre-forward, who proceeded to net what turned out to be the only goal of the game.

The players' heads went down, and an air of despondency set in on the team. One stupid mistake had undone the game plan. To say that manager McPherson was livid was an understatement. He was positively fuming.

131

As a consequence, Wastby Wanderers were leap-frogged by Ferryport, who went on to win the league championship by one point after both clubs, as had been predicted, won their two remaining fixtures.

Robbie Falconer was held responsible for the Wanderers' failure to win the title, and was consequently dropped from the first eleven. Unsurprisingly, he was released by the club at the end of the season; not only for that one crucial error, but for his general attitude towards the club and its officials.

With his reputation having gone before him, Robbie was now regarded as a 'loose cannon', and no other professional side was interested in his signature. He had no other option than to resume playing in the non-professional leagues, and was subsequently re-instated as an amateur with Seadykes Athletic.

Willie Wilson, on the other hand, went on to greater things. After a second season with Wastby, during which his prolific goal-scoring exploits continued unabated, albeit with a new striking partner, his dream of playing at the highest level came true when he was transferred to one of the top English sides for a substantial fee. Willie's football career continued to go from strength to strength, and eventually the international selectors came calling.

Meanwhile, back in Seadykes, Robbie Falconer was spending his days ruminating about what might have been.

True, he was back playing for his hometown club and knocking in the goals, but that gave him nowhere near the thrill that he got playing professional football in front of thousands of spectators.

One cold, damp and miserable Monday morning, after having drained the dregs from his tea cup and pushed his chair back from the breakfast table, Robbie stood up and pulled on his coat.

His father, seated opposite, was reading the morning paper.

"Have ye seen the sports headline this morning?" his father enquired, knowing only full well that his son would have scanned the back page not long after the paper had dropped through the letter box.

Robbie sighed. "Yes. Yes I have. I've seen it."

As if to rub salt in the wound, Robbie's dad read the headline out aloud.

"Willie Wilson To Make Scotland Debut".

Robbie shook his head, lifted his kit bag and headed towards the door.

"Aye, that could hae been you" his father said as Robbie turned the door handle. "That could hae been you that wis tae pull on the dark blue o' Scotland. But no, you always knew better than anybody else. You just wouldn't take a tellin'. You always had tae cut aff yer nose tae spite yer face".

Robbie said nothing. He went through the front door and out into the cold and damp morning, slung his kit bag over his shoulder, and started to make his way down to the harbour.

The End

If you enjoyed this book, you might also enjoy:

Dyker Lad:
Recollections of Life in an East Neuk of Fife Fishing Village

ISBN: 9781981019137

A
Selection of Poems
by
'Poetry Peter'
Smith

the Fisherman Poet
of Cellardyke

ISBN: 9798644727827

Both of the above titles are available in both paperback and Kindle eBook format from: Amazon.co.uk

Other Publications available from Wast-By Books:

East of Thornton Junction: The Story of the FifeCoast Line

(James K. Corstorphine, 1995)

ISBN: 9781976909283

On That Windswept Plain: The First One Hundred Years of East Fife Football Club

(James K. Corstorphine, 2003)

ISBN: 9781976888618

The Earliest Fife Football Clubs

(James K. Corstorphine, 2018)

ISBN: 9781980249580

Our Boys and the Wise Men: The Origins of Dundee Football Club

(James K. Corstorphine, 2020)

ISBN: 9798643521549

All of the above titles are available in both Paperback and Kindle eBook formats from:

amazon.co.uk

Just one more thing before you go . . .

Your opinion would be very much appreciated!

I would be most grateful if you could find a few minutes to rate this book on Amazon.

I will take the time to read any comments made, and any suggestions as to how I can improve the publication will be taken on board.

Thank you!

James Kingscott

Printed in Great Britain
by Amazon

53350733R00081